HER KIND OF HERO

CINDY KIRK

Copyright © Cynthia Rutledge 2020

All rights reserved.

No part of this book may be reproduced in any form or by any electronic or mechanical means, including information storage and retrieval systems, without written permission from the author, except for the use of brief quotations in a book review.

This is a work of fiction. Names, characters, places and incidents are products of the author's imagination or are used fictitiously. Any resemblance to actual events, locales, organizations, or persons, living or dead, is entirely coincidental.

ISBN: 9798649609449

First published in 2014 as THE HUSBAND LIST by Silhouette Books

CHAPTER ONE

The home in the mountains, decorated for fall, now included a banner above the fireplace proclaiming Welcome Home, Keenan. Across the room, a large buffet table held generous portions of everything from brisket to wedges of key lime pie. Travis Fisher and his wife, Mary Karen, had pulled out all the stops for this welcome-home party. Or rather, a get-out-of-prison celebration.

Waiters in black pants and crisp white shirts circulated throughout the house holding silver trays with hors d'oeuvres and champagne.

Dr. Mitzi Sanchez turned down the dumplings and baby quiche then took a glass of wine from a passing waiter before stepping into a secluded alcove to study the scene before her. Since moving to Wyoming three years ago, she'd been to a lot of parties in Jackson Hole.

While it appeared most in attendance had come with someone, she'd arrived alone. Her last guy, an NFL football player, had been more of a fling. Even in a casual relationship she required monogamy, and that hadn't been in Kelvin's playbook.

Across the room she saw her associate, Dr. Benedict Campbell, and his wife, Poppy. Of all her relationships, he'd lasted the longest. While on paper they should have been perfect for each other, they'd argued constantly. After they broke up, he'd begun dating Poppy and was now a happily married man with an adorable baby boy.

She didn't want a baby—not quite ready for that commitment—but she would like to be happily-with-someone. Mitzi heaved a sigh.

"That's quite a sigh."

She turned toward the sexy baritone and her heart stuttered. With hair the color of rich mahogany and hazel eyes that tended toward green, Mitzi found the man's square jaw and strong features pleasing. He smelled of soap and a familiar warm male scent that made something tighten low in her abdomen.

"Hel-lo." Mitzi widened her smile and let the word hum between them.

Because Keenan McGregor—the man they were welcoming home—had grown up in Jackson Hole, Travis had invited friends from his school years. Many of whom Mitzi had never met.

Still, Mitzi thought she knew every attractive man in Jackson Hole. "How did I miss seeing you?"

"You were too busy ogling the buffet table."

"I was not—" she began, then stopped when a dimple flashed in his left cheek. The rat was teasing her.

"Actually I was checking out who was here." She lowered her voice as she spoke, forcing him to lean close. Mitzi saw his eyes darken as he inhaled the sultry scent of her new perfume.

She took a sip of champagne. This party might be fun, after all. She batted her lashes then extended her hand. "Mitzi Sanchez."

His hand closed around hers and she felt a jolt. She glanced up, stunned by her response. If he'd experienced the same sizzle it didn't show.

"A pretty name for a lovely woman."

Though it was a compliment any reasonably attractive

HER KIND OF HERO | 3

woman would hear in a bar any night of the week, he offered it up with such sincerity, Mitzi felt herself smiling back. When his gaze slowly slid down her body, the earlier sizzle ignited into a full-out electrical fire.

Too fast, Mitzi told herself. *Take a step back.* They'd been words to live by and had kept her from making a few disastrous mistakes through the years.

Deliberately, she shifted her gaze to where their blonde hostess, Mary Karen, stood surrounded by friends, talking animatedly with both hands. Instead of her normal jeans and sweater, MK looked adorable in a royal blue sweater dress with a shawl neckline.

Mary Karen had told everyone the party would be casual. For this crowd that meant anything from jeans to fall dresses and heels. Though the hunk beside her looked mouthwateringly good in Wranglers and a wheat-colored sweater, Mitzi enjoyed dressing up almost as much as she liked changing her hair.

For tonight's event, she'd chosen a corduroy skirt in camel and a crisp cotton shirt in pumpkin spice. Her hair, which changed color so much she couldn't quite recall the original shade, was blond tonight with streaks the color of peanut butter. In a whimsical mood, she'd pulled the sides back and secured the strands with two of her favorite clips.

"You have bones in your hair."

Feeling more in control, Mitzi turned back to him and gave a throaty laugh. "They're femurs."

"Why do you have femurs in your hair?"

"I'm an orthopedic surgeon," Mitzi explained. "I found these hair clips at an eclectic little boutique in L.A. I pull them out for special occasions."

He took a sip of the drink in his hand, which looked like water but may have been vodka. Shadows played in his eyes, making them unreadable. "Tonight is special?"

"It is for Keenan McGregor. The guy got a get-out-of-jail-free card after being convicted of manslaughter." Mitzi lifted her glass of champagne as if making a toast. "A cause for celebration if I ever heard one. Don't you agree?"

"Definitely." His lips curved slightly upward. "An orthopedic surgeon? My arm was broken when I was ten so I guess we have that in common."

Even with a glass of champagne in her hand and a handsome man at her side, Mitzi still wore her doctor's hat. He'd said his arm *was broken* rather than he broke his arm. If he'd been a child, the wording would have put her on alert. But the man before her was definitely no boy.

"The last thing I want to do when I come to a party is talk about medicine. Let's chat about something more interesting." She stepped closer. "Such as you."

He didn't retreat, merely took another sip of his drink. "I'm not all that interesting."

Oh, but he was. His rugged good looks and confident demeanor called to her in a primal way and made her determined to uncover all his secrets.

Unable to resist touching him for one more second, Mitzi looped a hand through his arm. "You're just being modest. C'mon, tell me something about yourself."

"I love to fly."

"Are you a pilot?"

"I was." His eyes turned dark. "I'm working on getting my license back. That's at the top of my list."

Mitzi thought of her own list, the one she'd compiled just that morning. After years of playing the field, she was finally ready to settle down. Her list detailed essential characteristics she required in a husband. No more wasting time dating the wrong kind of men. "I have one of those."

"A pilot's license?"

The question flummoxed her. Then she chuckled. "No. A list."

"What's on yours?"

"Nuh-uh." She waggled a finger at him. "We're not talking about me. We're talking about you. I don't even know your name."

"Tell me one thing first." His slow, easy smile did strange things to her insides. "How do you happen to be at this party? You're not from Jackson Hole."

"I'm from California." Not about to be distracted, Mitzi steered the conversation back to him. "I take it you're from here?"

He nodded, shifted his gaze from her.

"Since you were invited, you must know Keenan."

Those beautiful hazel eyes returned to her. "Extremely well."

"Point him out." Mitzi tightened her grip on his arm. "I've been trying to figure out which one he is but it's difficult. I know Betsy, but some siblings don't resemble each other."

She thought of her sister, who looked one hundred percent like their Mexican mother, while Mitzi took after her Argentinean father with her blue eyes and fair complexion.

"True enough." He brushed back a lock of hair that fell sexily across his forehead.

Her body began to thrum. Mitzi had to force her eyes from his face to scan the crowd. "Can I see him from where I'm standing?"

"You can."

"Tell me." She lowered her voice to a conspiratorial whisper. "Which one is the convict?"

He tipped her chin up with his finger until her eyes met his. "You're looking at him."

For a fraction of a second, Mitzi's blue eyes widened. Then, she laughed. "Yeah, right."

Keenan wasn't sure why he found the conversation amusing,

but he did. "I'd show you my driver's license but it expired when I was in prison."

She was a pretty thing, and unlike any doctor he'd ever known. Not that he ran in that crowd. Or rather, he hadn't in the past. Coming back to Jackson Hole, it had surprised him that so many of his boyhood pals were now important members of the medical community.

"You're not Keenan McGregor." Though she spoke boldly, confidently, the uncertainty in her eyes told him she wasn't so sure. "You're making it up."

"Travis." He gestured his friend over.

The popular ob-gyn, tall and lean with sandy-colored hair and a perpetual smile, sauntered toward them.

Travis had been one of a group of men who'd worked tirelessly for Keenan's release and provided money for his legal fees. Though his friends insisted he didn't owe them a dime, Keenan had vowed to repay every penny, no matter how long it took.

"I see you've met Mitzi." Travis's smile broadened to include the woman at his side.

"We're getting acquainted." Keenan shot Mitzi a wink. "I was just telling her I don't have a driver's license since mine expired while I was in prison."

"You're going to need one." Travis rocked back on his heels. "I understand you'll be working with Joel while you get back on your feet."

Although Keenan had only recently met Travis's friend, Joel had offered him a job with his construction company. "I appreciate the opportunity."

Travis's eyes took on a distant look. "You were always fooling around with wood or engines when we were growing up."

Out of necessity, Keenan thought with a wry smile. He'd had to keep the old jalopy he'd driven running, and if he hadn't done repairs to the dump of a house where they'd lived, it would have fallen in around them.

"Thanks for the party, Trav." Keenan gestured toward the room filled with family and old friends. "You and Mary Karen went to a lot of trouble to pull this together."

"We're happy to have you back." The sincerity in Travis's eyes humbled Keenan. He'd done little to deserve such loyalty. "If you need anything, anything at all—"

"You've done enough already." Keenan clasped a hand on his friend's shoulder. "But thanks. I appreciate the offer."

They talked for another minute before Travis left to answer a catering question. It wasn't until after he disappeared into the crowd that Keenan turned back to Mitzi, who'd been messing with her smartphone while undoubtedly listening to every word. "Satisfied?"

Instead of looking abashed, she grinned. "You were right."

"About being me?"

"I had my doubts." Mitzi looked him up and down, sizing him up. "You and Betsy don't really look alike."

Before he could respond, she spun on her heel. "I'm getting something to eat. Perhaps snag more champagne. I'm not on call so I'm allowing myself two glasses this evening."

Keenan used to drink, quite a bit during high school and even more during the following years. Then he quit. Not because alcohol was a problem for him, but because he didn't want it to become one.

He watched her saunter off and felt a stab of disappointment. Hanging out with her had been fun...while it lasted.

"Hey." Mitzi turned, cast a challenging glance over her shoulder. "Aren't you coming?"

Growing up in East Los Angeles, Mitzi had plenty of experience with convicts. Her mother had dated many and had even lived with a few of them. Her sister had married one. Or was it two?

Such relationships never ended well. Mitzi, who'd been determined to get out of that life and never look back, had never been remotely attracted to someone who'd had trouble with the law.

Of course, Keenan had been sent to prison for a crime he hadn't committed. That still didn't mean he was the kind of man she'd be interested in dating.

She wanted a successful man, someone with a lot of drive and ambition. From what she'd heard, Keenan had been living a hedonistic lifestyle before he landed in jail. Still, she enjoyed talking with him. What would be the harm in chatting a little while longer over a crab cake or two?

"Did I offend you with the convict comment?" she asked when he joined her.

"I am a convict." Keenan shrugged. "I spent time in prison. Granted, I didn't kill the guy, but I was still convicted and sent away."

"True."

On their way to the buffet table, they were stopped every few feet by someone wanting to hug Keenan or offer congratulations.

He handled the attention well, Mitzi noticed. Keenan had an easy charm and a ready smile, but she could feel the tension in the arm she held and knew this light mood wasn't as effortless for him as it appeared.

"This must be difficult," she said, when they finally reached the table.

"I'm not used to the social thing anymore," Keenan said with a slightly abashed look. "Still it's nice knowing so many people care."

Mitzi wondered if she'd inspire such loyalty, then shoved the thought aside. She had more important things on her mind right now. She slanted a sideways glance at Keenan. "Do you like crab cakes?"

He tilted his head. "Is that a trick question?"

"I want a bite of one but not the whole thing."

HER KIND OF HERO | 9

"You could, I don't know, leave the part you don't want on your plate."

Mitzi had spent many years in a household without enough to eat. She could be wasteful in a lot of areas of her life, but food wasn't one of them. Wrinkling her nose, she shook her head.

His lips twitched. "Since that obviously isn't an acceptable option, I'll be a gentleman and help you out."

With a satisfied smirk, Mitzi dropped a crab cake on the plate. "If you only want a bite of something, I'll do the same."

"I'm not a guy who does things halfway."

Something told her he wasn't joking.

When he reached for his own plate, she put a hand on his arm, shook her head. "We'll share."

Amusement flickered in his eyes. "Anyone ever tell you that you're bossy?"

"All the time." She snatched a deep-fried ball of something from a tray and popped it into her mouth.

Rolling his eyes, he did the same. Chewed. Swallowed. "Tasty."

"Better than prison food?"

"Much better," he agreed.

They made their way down the long table, her pointing to something and him shaking his head, then repeating the process with him doing the pointing. By the time they finished, the plate was full.

Though Mitzi had just met Keenan, conversation flowed freely. They didn't talk about medicine or theater events or fancy wines, but about food and now, cats.

"Mr. Tubs wasn't anything special." Keenan finished off the crab cake Mitzi had sliced in half with surgical precision. "But he was a good mouser and smart as a whip. Betsy and I even taught him tricks. Believe me, that wasn't easy to do."

Mitzi heard the affection, knew the animal had been special. "I had a cat, Oreo. I found her abandoned in a Dumpster. Like your Tubs, she earned a place in the household by keeping the mice population down."

"What happened to her?"

Mitzi lifted one shoulder. "She got old. One day we opened the door and she slipped out. I read cats often go away to die. I like to think that's what happened to her."

Keenan nodded, lifted a mozzarella stick from the plate.

"What happened to Tubs?"

His lips tightened. "My mother sold him."

Just the way he said *mother* told Mitzi there wasn't any love between them.

"Why did she do that?"

"Like I said, he could do tricks." Keenan looked down at the mozzarella stick as if trying to figure out what was in his hand. "She needed money for booze. We came home from school and Tubs was gone. She didn't remember—she said—who bought him. It was...difficult. Betsy was devastated."

From the look in Keenan's eyes, his sister hadn't been the only one. Mitzi took the mozzarella stick from his hand, dropped it onto the plate then set it aside. "Let's take a walk."

When they got to the back of the house, he reached around her to open the French doors leading to a deck festively lit with party lights. Couples stood in small, intimate groups talking and laughing under the golden glow from a full moon. The crisp scent of dried leaves mingled with the pungent aroma of evergreen.

After speaking briefly with several friends and getting hugs from a few more, Keenan moved to the rail and inhaled deeply. "So many times I wondered if I'd ever have this again."

"Well, now you're back."

"And starting over." He paused, shook his head as if clearing it. "That's inaccurate. I'm beginning the next phase in my life. Out with the old. In with the new."

That's exactly how Mitzi had felt when she'd gone to college.

Moving on. Leaving the past behind. Except she'd discovered the past often came with you, even without a proper invitation.

"What is that?" Keenan's question pulled her from her reverie.

Mitzi turned, caught her breath at his nearness. With great effort she forced her attention to where he pointed. Someone had tied a sprig of berries to an overhanging branch. She smiled. "It's mistletoe."

Keenan cocked his head, looking perplexed. "Why would mistletoe be hanging from a tree branch in September?"

"It's kind of a tradition." Mitzi explained how Travis and Mary Karen had mistletoe at all their parties, regardless of the time of year.

He stared at the berries and waxy green leaves, then lifted a brow.

The moment his eyes touched hers, something inside seemed to lock into place, and Mitzi couldn't look away. Her lips began to tingle with anticipation. From the expression of watchful waiting in his eyes, it was clear he wouldn't make the first move.

Though Keenan McGregor wasn't someone she could see herself dating, kissing wasn't dating. It was, well, just kissing.

It could be a glad-you're-finally-out-of-prison kiss, a way of welcoming him back to Jackson Hole. It didn't need to be complicated.

Without giving herself time to talk herself out of the impulsive gesture, Mitzi wrapped her arms around his neck and lifted her mouth to his.

CHAPTER TWO

Before her lips could meet his, Keenan gently but firmly moved Mitzi back from him. Her eyes, which had started to close, flew open. "Wha—"

"I didn't want you to feel obligated." He gestured with his head toward the berries.

Mitzi rarely blushed, but she recognized the heat crawling up her neck. She couldn't remember the last time a guy had turned away one of her kisses or she'd been so completely impulsive.

Impulsive, most certainly. Completely impulsive, no.

"You're right." She flashed him a bright smile. "I don't know what came over me."

He skimmed his knuckles down her cheek. "I don't know what it is, either, but it's damn enticing."

The gentle touch reignited the desire hovering just below the surface. Darn if she was going to make another move on him.

She didn't have to because, before Mitzi could utter a word, he cupped her face in his hands and kissed her with surprising tenderness. His lips were warm against hers, and he tasted of spearmint.

HER KIND OF HERO | 13

Confused—and slightly dazed—Mitzi glanced up at him. He must have seen the question in her eyes.

"We kissed," he said, in a low rumbling tone that made her belly jitter, "because we wanted to kiss. Not because of berries and leaves."

Which meant she couldn't blame her response on the mistletoe. Maybe a little on the full moon hanging like a large golden orb in the sky. Or on the intoxicating way he smelled. Or simply because she wanted to see what it was like to kiss an ex-con.

She jerked back at the realization of whom she'd just locked lips with, whom she'd enjoyed locking lips with, whom she wanted to kiss again.

Red flags popped up so fast it made her dizzy. After her football-player fling, Mitzi had promised herself she'd get serious about finding Mr. Right. She'd agonized over the criteria that had to be met before she would consider a guy relationship material.

After all, she had a gene pool trying to pull her down. From the time she was a teenager, she'd found herself drawn to boys who liked having fun a whole lot more than they liked studying. Guys with flash but no substance.

Guys like Keenan McGregor? She didn't know him well enough to make such a judgment, yet how could she not? It was a self-preservation kind of thing.

Unlike her sister, who now had three kids by three different men, Mitzi's vision for her future never included struggling for every penny or having a kid before she was out of high school.

She'd stuck to the straight and narrow. Studied, worked hard and got out. Her life was just as she liked it. Mitzi wasn't going to let anyone—even a handsome ex-con—pull her off course.

∾

Keenan saw it in the beautiful blue eyes the second she dismissed him. He wasn't sure why she'd wanted to kiss him—though he knew she had—when he obviously wasn't her usual kind of guy.

Understanding didn't stop the twinge of regret that settled like a lump of clay in his belly. Something told him, given the chance, they'd have enjoyed each other's company.

Keenan reminded himself Mitzi wasn't the only woman in Jackson Hole. If he was looking for a woman. Which he was not. He'd barely arrived back in town. He hadn't even had time to unpack the bag sitting in his sister's guest bedroom.

On Monday, he'd start his construction job. When he got off work, he'd look for a place to stay so he didn't inconvenience his sister and brother-in-law any further. Despite Ryan and Betsy's assurance that he was welcome to stay indefinitely, the desire to make his own way, to begin to rebuild the life he'd lost, was a burning need inside him.

"I suppose—" Mitzi began.

"I should mingle." Keenan shoved his hands into his pockets, forcing a calm tone. He let his gaze skim over her once more then smiled. "It was good getting to know you. Thanks for the welcome-home kiss."

Before he could embarrass himself by telling her to give him a call if she was ever free or something equally lame, he shot her a wink and sauntered back inside.

Mitzi watched in stunned disbelief as the man she'd been prepared to brush off opened the French doors and disappeared from view. Her impromptu speech of dismissal had been fully formed on her lips but he'd spoken first.

Irritation bubbled inside her. She clenched her hands into fists. He'd not only walked off, he had the audacity to wink at her.

Well, no man walked away from Mitzi Sanchez in such a

HER KIND OF HERO | 15

cavalier manner. She was going to go inside, seek him out and tell him to his face that—

She paused, even in her anger realizing the irrationality of her plan. What could she say to him that wouldn't make her sound like a kook? Or worse yet, desperate?

Taking a couple of deep, steadying breaths, Mitzi turned back to the rail and gazed over the lush lawn. Deep in her thoughts, she didn't immediately notice that her friend, Kate Dennes, now stood beside her.

"You're quite the party animal tonight." Kate rested her hands on the rail and cast a sidelong glance in Mitzi's direction.

"I needed air."

"I saw you stroll out here with Keenan." Kate's expression gave nothing away. "Then he came back inside alone."

"He wanted to mingle." Mitzi could have cheered when her voice came out calm and offhand. "I preferred to stay out here a little longer."

Kate nudged Mitzi with her elbow. "He's quite a hunk."

Mitzi lifted a shoulder in a little shrug. "I suppose. If you like the type."

The smile faded from Kate's lips. "Type?"

"Arrogant." The moment the word slipped past Mitzi's lips, she felt a pang of regret. As if she'd said something bad about a friend. Then she reminded herself that Keenan wasn't a friend. He wasn't anything more than a guy she had kissed under a full moon.

Kate inhaled sharply. "I hope that won't be a problem."

Mitzi shifted her body toward her friend, cocked her head.

"Joel hired him on the basis of everyone's recommendation." Kate chewed on her lip. "Customer service and teamwork is important to him. If Keenan has a bad attitude..."

Mitzi knew there were no secrets between Kate and her contractor husband, Joel. Once Kate was alone with her spouse, she'd share what Mitzi had told her. Keenan would

16 | CINDY KIRK

have one strike against him before he even started his new job.

That would be my fault.

"He's not really arrogant," Mitzi said quickly, then felt heat rise up her neck at Kate's assessing look.

"That's what you said."

"We kissed then he walked away as if it meant nothing," Mitzi huffed. "Pissed me off."

The serious look in Kate's eyes faded, replaced by something that resembled amusement. "Did you say you kissed him?"

Mitzi scowled. "Is something wrong with your hearing?"

"You just met."

"*Kissed,* Kate," Mitzi sputtered. "I didn't hop into bed with him."

Kate searched Mitzi's eyes then gave a little laugh. "You wanted to."

Mitzi started to deny it then chuckled. "He's hot." She lifted a shoulder in a slight shrug. "Just not my type."

"Please don't tell me you're still focused on that football player."

Mitzi took a glass of champagne a passing waiter offered, and then enjoyed one delicious sip before answering. "That cheating snake? Get real. I'm not about to chase one mistake with another."

Kate took a sip from the glass of water she'd brought with her to the deck. "You believe becoming involved with Keenan would be a mistake."

"He's an ex-con, Kate."

"Innocent of all charges."

"I'm looking for a different kind of man. Someone more like Winn Ferris or..." Mitzi brought a finger to her lips. "Tim Duggan."

Tim Duggan was a physician in the same OB-GYN practice as

HER KIND OF HERO | 17

their mutual friend, Travis Fisher. A widower with twin girls, the young doctor kept a low profile in the community.

"I like Tim." Kate spoke slowly, as if choosing her words carefully. "He and I served on a medical-ethics committee together last year, so I got to know him pretty well. I'd be happy to set you up. I have to say, you and he don't seem like a particularly good fit."

"Why?" Mitzi bristled. "Because he went to some Ivy League school and I grew up in East L.A.?"

Something in Kate's eyes flickered, but her expression didn't alter. "Because he's quiet and very family oriented. His life revolves around his daughters."

Mitzi considered. Dating a man with kids wouldn't be her first choice, but she could adjust. "I could be family oriented."

She didn't even bother with the "quiet." Keeping her mouth shut had never been a strength.

"In all the time you've lived in Jackson, you've never once given Tim a second glance. It doesn't make sense that all of a sudden you're hot for him."

"I'm *interested* in getting to know him better." Mitzi's tone stopped just short of petulant. "I'm tired of dating the wrong men. I'm not getting any younger and I need to focus on quality."

"Benedict Campbell was quality," Kate reminded her. "You focused on him for well over a year."

"Ben was—is—a quality guy," Mitzi concurred. "But all we did was argue. He's quite arrogant."

Kate sipped her water. "*Arrogant.* There's that word again."

"You know he is," Mitzi insisted.

"Poppy doesn't seem to think so." Kate gestured with her head.

Mitzi realized with a start that the couple standing so close together on the far end of the large deck was indeed her former flame and his wife. His arm was wrapped around her waist and her head rested against his shoulder.

18 | CINDY KIRK

"They seem happy together," Mitzi grudgingly admitted. "What's the point here? Are you implying *I'm* the one who's difficult?"

"I'm saying," Kate's tone remained low and even, "that you've dated all sorts of men. You simply haven't found the right one."

"That's why I made a list," Mitzi confided, pleased with herself for taking this proactive step. "Wrote down all the qualities I want in a husband."

Kate didn't appear surprised. She probably recalled the lists Mitzi had made all through residency. Lists of manners she needed to master so as to not embarrass herself in public. Lists of things she needed to learn about everything from wine to art.

"What kept Keenan McGregor off the list?"

Mitzi took another sip of champagne. The qualities that she'd listed had been well thought out and valid. Yet, somehow, the thought of saying them aloud made her uneasy.

She reminded herself she hadn't gotten to where she was in life by caring what other people thought.

"Successful." Mitzi met Kate's gaze. "I want a man who's achieved a certain measure of success by the time he's reached his thirties. While I admit Keenan is good-looking and charming, he's certainly not, by anyone's measure, a success."

"You're wrong."

Mitzi whirled.

Betsy Harcourt, Keenan's sister, stood so close it was obvious that while Mitzi had kept her voice deliberately low, the woman had heard every word.

Mitzi flinched. "I didn't mean for you—"

"Don't." With a finger pointed directly at Mitzi, Betsy spoke, her voice snapping like a whip. "Don't say another word."

Stunned, Mitzi obeyed. This was a side to the sweet and docile paralegal she'd never seen. The sprinkle of freckles across Betsy's nose now stood like angry pennies against the pallor of her skin.

HER KIND OF HERO | 19

"You're wrong about Keenan. Dead wrong. My brother *is* a success. Perhaps he doesn't have a shiny red sports car or a big house in Spring Gulch, but he's successful in the ways that matter." Betsy's eyes flashed a warning when Mitzi started to open her mouth.

"Keenan raised me when he was only a kid himself. Never did he make me feel like a burden. He went to prison to protect me. Gave up his freedom for me." Betsy brought her clenched fist to her chest. "If you can't see that Keenan is a special guy, then I'm telling you...stay away from him. He deserves only good things— and good people—in his life."

Tears welled in Betsy's blue eyes. Before they could fall, the brunette blinked them back and straightened her shoulders. She shifted her focus to Kate, who stood slack-jawed at Mitzi's side. "Mary Karen needs to speak with you."

"I'll be right in," Kate responded when she finally found her voice, but Betsy had already spun on her heel and was headed inside.

Sighing, Mitzi bit her lip. "That was awful."

Kate nodded. "I'm afraid it's only going to get more so, at least for you."

Mitzi cocked her head.

"The man you were just told to steer clear of is going to be the one trimming out your new home."

CHAPTER THREE

Keenan glanced around the family room of the gracious home in the Spring Gulch subdivision of Jackson Hole. At just over 2,100 square feet, Mitzi's home might not be as large as some, but the spacious interior and the stone and brick exterior was appealing and surprisingly cozy.

After spending the morning raising rafters on a house in the mountains, he was sent by Joel to help Bill on Mitzi's home. It was the first Keenan had seen of the place. "It's a beauty."

"Turning out nice." Balding and somewhere in his fifties, the foreman reminded Keenan of an accountant.

Buckling on the tool belt Joel had lent him, Keenan studied the French doors leading to a vaulted screened porch. Though he thought the house was still an awful lot of space for one person, he admired the efficiency of the floor plan. "For some reason I thought Mitzi, er, Dr. Sanchez, had a condo."

"She bought a place in Teton Village about a year ago. She didn't like it." Bill shrugged. "Being an orthopedic surgeon, the lady has money to burn."

Money to burn.

HER KIND OF HERO | 21

Keenan wondered what that would be like. Right now he'd be satisfied with enough cash to last until his next paycheck.

"Does she come around much?" He kept his tone casual.

"Every couple of days she drives up in that little red BMW M6." Bill sanded a piece of trim. "Friendly enough. Stays just long enough to check on the progress. Sometimes asks a few questions. That's about it. She's a real looker."

"She certainly is."

Curiosity sparked in the older man's eyes. "You acquainted?"

"We met recently." Keenan measured a piece of molding and made a quick cut with the miter box. "She knows people I know."

"Gabe and Joel are both married to doctors."

Keenan was well aware of that fact. Joel, owner of Stone Craft Builders, was married to Mitzi's good friend, Kate. He'd briefly met Gabe Davis, the construction engineer who was Joel's second in command. Keenan hadn't yet met Gabe's wife, Michelle, another local doctor.

"Speak of the devil." Bill brushed some of the sawdust off his pants and straightened.

Keenan followed Bill's gaze out the front window and saw a car pull to a stop in the driveway. Mitzi got out and straightened a skirt the color of the Wyoming sky, modest but short enough to reveal an enticing expanse of tanned and toned thighs.

Keenan wasn't sure if it was the legs or the cream-colored sweater hugging her generous curves that made his insides jiggle like the gelatin Betsy served for dessert last night.

He frowned. What was it about Mitzi that made him feel like some geeky teen crushing on the school's head cheerleader?

Best not to delve too deeply into that muddy pool, he told himself. What mattered was the last time they were together he'd brushed off the gorgeous doctor. He'd done to her before she could do to him. The realization that he hadn't let his attraction to her tie him into knots buoyed his courage. When the front door opened and Mitzi stepped inside, the smile he shot her was easy.

Her own smile flashed warm and friendly. If she felt any discomfort over seeing him again, it didn't show.

"Dr. Sanchez." Bill stepped forward. As the job site foreman, working with the client was his responsibility when Joel or Gabe wasn't there. "We're making good progress."

"C'mon, Bill. Please call me Mitzi." She slanted a sideways glance at Keenan. "Hello, again."

Keenan touched the brim of his ball cap. "Ma'am."

She frowned then turned from him in dismissal. Her imperious gaze swept the room.

He tried to see the home through her eyes: the massive stone fireplace with hand-carved mantel against one wall, twelve-foot ceilings that pulled the eyes upward, creating a feeling of openness. Whoever had drawn up the plans had done a superb job of contrasting warmth and comfort with understated elegance.

"I'm going to wander." She waved a hand. "Don't let me disturb you."

"I can show you—" Bill began then glanced down as the phone clipped to his belt buzzed. He lifted it, grimaced. "I'm afraid I need to take this. Keenan can point out what we've finished up today."

"I don't need—"

"I'm happy to do it," Keenan said smoothly, catching Bill's look.

Mitzi must have noticed it too, because she didn't protest further.

"Bill set the countertop this morning." He gestured with one hand as they entered the kitchen area. Keenan pointed out several other accomplishments Bill had mentioned when he'd first arrived.

Though Mitzi listened intently, she didn't say much. As the

HER KIND OF HERO | 23

tour continued, he understood by the way her gaze kept flitting to him and lingering that lust had punched her, too. Desire, hot as a fired-up grill, snapped and sizzled in the air.

She might be determined to push him away—as he was with her—but he'd stake his life she was fighting a losing battle with the pull.

No guts. No glory.

His former mantra rose up and slapped him in the face.

"Do you have plans for dinner?" Keenan heard himself ask when they paused at the door to the last of the three bedrooms.

Her head swiveled.

"I was thinking of stopping by Perfect Pizza tonight." He gave a careless shrug. Just because he'd succumbed to the urge didn't mean he'd beg. "Interested?"

Mitzi slid a hand along the recently sanded doorjamb and his mouth went dry.

Okay, maybe he'd consider begging.

"Interested?" She lifted a brow. "In what?"

In pushing up that sweater and letting me fill my hands with your breasts.

In tugging that scrap of skirt down and exploring with my mouth and tongue what lies beneath.

Heck, yes, he was interested.

Keenan took a moment to collect himself. "Pizza, of course."

"I'm not sure us having dinner is a good idea."

Keenan understood. Right now his own gut roiled. But standing back and letting life happen had never been his style. He gave a little chuckle. "You're afraid."

"Don't be silly." She huffed. "I'm not afraid of anything. Or anyone."

He clucked like a chicken, a noise straight from childhood. It had infuriated Betsy when he'd used it on her as a kid. From the flash of temper in Mitzi's eyes, it had the same effect on her.

"Have you considered," she said between gritted teeth, "that I simply may not want to share a pizza with you but am too polite to say so?"

"Nope. Absolutely not." He shook his head. "Chicken."

Her lips twitched upward. Just once.

"If I did come," she began, waving one hand loosely in the air, "it would be because I'm hungry. And because I haven't had...pizza...in weeks."

"Understood." He hadn't had...pizza...in years, either.

"It wouldn't be a date," she said quickly. "And I won't allow you to pay my share."

"Hmm." Keenan rubbed his chin. "I don't recall offering."

Her eyes narrowed to slits. She didn't even crack a smile. "I'll be blunt. I'm not looking for a relationship with you."

"Sheesh, Mitzi." Keenan lifted his hands, palms out. "Way to blow a simple invite into the stratosphere."

She blew out a breath. "As long as we understand each other."

Though she did a good job of hiding it, he saw the desire lurking in her eyes. Ah, yes, they understood each other. Quite well, in fact.

He fixed his gaze on her, let it drop and linger on her breasts before returning to her lips. "I know exactly what I want."

"Oh, yeah? Well, tonight what you're going to get is pizza."

He hid a grin, wondering if Mitzi realized that instead of slamming the door shut, she'd left it slightly ajar.

Mitzi told herself if she didn't find a parking space on the first pass through downtown, she'd head to Hill of Beans, pick up a nice Cobb salad and take it home to eat.

As she sped down Main, an Escalade eased from the curb, leaving a space big enough for the entire state of Utah. Yet, even after she pulled into the spot, Mitzi made no move to get out.

When she'd left Keenan and Bill at her new home, it hadn't even been five. Now it was nearly seven. She'd had plenty of time to consider Keenan's dinner challenge. Even as she showered and changed her clothes, the red flags waving wildly in the air urged her to turn tail and run. It wouldn't be wise to meet him.

Not for pizza. Certainly not for sex.

Though if she was being totally honest, she'd have to admit to one or two lascivious thoughts when she'd seen him with that tool belt slung low across his hips and a white T-shirt stretched broad across his muscular chest.

Perhaps that's why she was here. To prove to herself she could still handle temptation. If she ever did hop into bed with him—and that was a mighty big *if*—it would be a rational decision, made after much thought.

It would be foolish and shortsighted to cast aside the option entirely. Her husband hunt could take time. Until she found someone who met her criteria, her choice was either to remain celibate or snatch a few moments of pleasure where she could find it.

It wasn't as if either she or Keenan would be using each other. Not if they both hopped into bed knowing it was only a physical thing. But tonight, the only thing on the menu was pizza.

Reassured, Mitzi headed for the restaurant.

Keenan spotted Mitzi before she saw him. Like him she wore jeans and a simple cotton shirt. But with heeled sandals and designer bag, the doctor looked anything but casual. In fact, with her hair tousled around her face, she looked like a stylish socialite who'd just tumbled out of bed after an afternoon of lovemaking.

In all his years as an adult male, Keenan couldn't remember ever wanting a woman the way he wanted Mitzi. When she drew close, his body began to hum. It wasn't just out-of-prison hormones but something deeper.

The tiny hairs at the base of his neck rose and electricity crackled in the air. Even knowing she didn't find him suitable for a "relationship" wasn't enough to quell the attraction.

That didn't mean he planned to sleep with her. Despite the teasing offer he'd extended, his years in the penitentiary had given him plenty of time to think. More important, time to assess where he came from and where he wanted to be headed.

Most of his life had been spent reacting, batting cleanup for his mother's wrong choices. Gloria's wild mood shifts, fueled by alcohol, had made a stable home life impossible. Still, for Betsy's sake, Keenan had tried.

He'd made dinner, even if it was only hot dogs or mac and cheese from a box. When a teacher had commented on the cleanliness of his clothes and he saw concern in her eyes, Keenan had figured out how to run the washer. He'd forced Betsy to take a shower every night and made her brush her hair before she left the house.

Keenan may not have had designer jeans or a closetful of clothes like most of his friends, but he and his sister were clean and stayed under the social service radar.

He knew some of the girls in his class considered him beneath them because he didn't have the cool car or the right clothes. Others had wanted him *because* of his bad-boy image. In their own way, both were snubs. Both had scraped bone. He'd assuaged pent-up fury with explosive contact during football games and later by participating in extreme sports.

Though he'd started to turn his life around before he was charged with murder, it was his prison counselor who helped him get his head straight.

She'd taught him to value his strengths, to not settle for less than he deserved. Keenan knew that being with a woman who considered him less than her, no matter how great the sex, would be settling.

When his body began to vibrate as Mitzi drew near, Keenan reminded himself that tonight only one thing was on the menu...pizza.

CHAPTER FOUR

Other than a group of giggly preteens and their parents, Perfect Pizza, a popular eatery in downtown Jackson, was surprisingly quiet. After placing their order at the counter, Mitzi picked up the table flag and plastic utensils. Keenan carried the glasses of soda to a series of wooden booths with high backs that lined the back wall.

Once seated, conversation flowed surprisingly easily. By the time the pizza was delivered to their table by a teenager in the throes of a war on acne, Mitzi had begun to relax.

Mitzi hesitated, not certain if she should eat the pizza with a fork or just pick it up. If she was alone she usually just picked up the slice.

When Keenan lifted his piece in one hand and took a bite, she relaxed and did the same.

The blend of herbs and spices, not to mention a generous artery-clogging supply of cheese, came together in something that could only be called delicious.

"I'm glad you like anchovies. Most people can't stand them," Keenan murmured, gazing at the large pie covered with the tiny fish on the table between them.

HER KIND OF HERO | 29

"They don't know what they're missing." Mitzi let the slice hover just beyond her lips then took another bite.

"That's true of most things in life," Keenan said, sounding surprisingly philosophical. "We don't try something because we don't think it will be good for us. Or we convince ourselves we won't like it even though we haven't tried it."

Mitzi pulled her brows together, unconvinced. "I don't have to go to prison to know I wouldn't like it."

The second the words left her mouth, she wished she could pull them back. It certainly wasn't her intent to keep ramming the fact that he'd spent the past few years behind bars down his throat.

Keenan took another bite of pizza, chewed. "You're right. Some things are no-brainers."

Though his tone was matter-of-fact, the light had faded from his eyes.

Impulsively Mitzi reached across the table and squeezed his hand. "I'm sorry."

"For what?"

She met his gaze firmly.

"Okay," he said. "So maybe all the prison comments are getting old."

"I'm sorry," she repeated. "Sincerely."

For several long seconds she let her hand rest on his. When he flipped his over and laced fingers with hers, her heart stumbled. His intensely passionate eyes suddenly looked more green than brown in the light.

"Let's talk about something more interesting," he said, his gaze never leaving hers. "Tell me about Mitzi Sanchez."

She moistened suddenly dry lips. "Not much to tell."

Her gaze dropped to their joined hands. She really should disengage.

Before she could make a move, his fingers tightened on hers

30 | CINDY KIRK

and his thumb began to stroke her palm. Inwardly, she shuddered.

"You told me that first night you were from California." Keenan's tone had a soothing effect. "I'd have pegged you as a California girl anyway. You have that free-spirit vibe."

Mitzi gave a little laugh. "I don't know whether to be offended or flattered."

"I meant it as a compliment." He tilted his head. "What part of the state?"

"Los Angeles," she answered then clarified, "East L.A."

"Tough area."

She quirked a brow. "You're familiar with the city?"

"I lived there for a while after I left Jackson."

Had he once hoped for a career on the big screen? He certainly had the looks, charm and a charisma that went beyond the physical. Mitzi tried to visualize Keenan waiting tables while hoping for a big break.

His sister was right. There was a quiet confidence about him, one that said here was a man who'd support, encourage, stick.

Shaking the ridiculous thought aside, Mitzi reminded herself she barely knew the guy. To make suppositions on limited information could be dangerous. "Were you a starving actor?"

"Starving MMA fighter," he said, then immediately switched the focus back to her. "Tell me how you ended up in Wyoming."

Mitzi resisted the urge to sigh. Though normally there was nothing she liked better than talking about herself, she was reluctant to share too much. Knowledge was power, after all. And like her, she sensed Keenan preferred to hold those reins.

Yet no matter how many times she tried to switch the conversation to him, he kept redirecting it back to her.

"I returned to California for my residency," she told him finally. "Kate and I met then, and we've been good friends ever since. She moved here and really liked it. When I finished my fellowship, there was an opening at Spring Gulch Orthopedics. They offered me the position, and here I am."

Instead of grabbing another slice of pizza, Keenan kept his entire attention on her. "Do you still have family in California?"

"My mother." Mitzi shifted in her seat, wishing the seats had more padding and Keenan would stop with the family questions. "A sister. Three nieces. What about you? I know your sister is here. What about your parents?"

A shadow passed over his face. "I don't remember my old man. He cut out shortly after Betsy was born. I was five. Gloria— our mother—died in a car accident several years back."

"I'm sorry to hear that—"

"She was drunk." His voice turned flat, his eyes now shuttered. "Police estimate she was going close to seventy when she hit the tree. Almost took out a kid on a bike."

Sympathy for the boy who'd grown up on his own washed over her even as the air filled with the bruised weight of the past.

"It's tough. My father died when I was seven." She surprised herself by revealing so much. But it felt right. "He was digging a trench when it caved in. He suffocated before they could get to him."

His gaze never left her face. "Heck of a way to go."

"Is there a good way?" Mitzi gave a careless shrug before pulling her hand from his and taking another slice of pizza.

They ate in companionable silence for several minutes. Mitzi found it odd she could be so relaxed in the company of a man she barely knew. Perhaps it was because she didn't feel the need to be anything but herself with him.

"Ben Campbell and I were on the same Little League team in grade school," Keenan said abruptly. "I heard the two of you dated for a while."

Mitzi raised a brow. "Plugged into the Jackson Hole gossip line already, McGregor?"

A quick grin flashed. "Hey, I can't help it if people want to catch me up to date."

"Then you should also be aware Ben is now a happily married man with a wife he loves and a bouncing baby boy."

"Wish it was you?"

"If I'd wanted it to be me, I'd have tried harder to make it work."

"If it don't come easy, best to let it go."

"Aren't you the philosophical one?"

His smile widened. "Just sayin' if you have to work at it so hard, perhaps it's not meant to be."

"If I subscribed to that theory, I'd still be back in L.A., cleaning houses like my mother or tending bar like my sister."

"Nothing wrong with honest labor," Keenan said mildly.

"There's also nothing wrong with having goals and trying to better yourself," she said casually. It was all she could do not to snap back at him.

"Is this where you get up and start preaching that everyone can succeed if they just try hard enough?"

There was something behind that bland expression, something in the way he said the words that told Mitzi if she did preach that sermon, he'd be the first to get up and leave. She called on her inner control and forced calmness to her voice she didn't feel. "You don't agree?"

He shrugged. "Does it matter?"

Let it go. His opinion didn't matter. She knew what she believed. Yet, she found herself saying, "Tell me."

He did. She listened—and ate—as Keenan spoke of the people he'd met before he'd gone to prison: decent hardworking men and women trying to build a better life for themselves and their families.

"When you get down so low, it's almost impossible to get out."

"Yeah, it's hard," Mitzi insisted. "Sacrifices have to be made."

"Did you work when you were in high school?"

HER KIND OF HERO | 33

"I worked my butt off. I cleaned houses. I scrubbed floors and toilets." She wrinkled her nose. "While my mother encouraged me to study, she'd have been satisfied to have me cleaning full-time after graduation. I was the one who wanted more."

"You were lucky," he said.

"Hardly." She gave a little laugh. "My bedroom in the new house is bigger than our entire apartment in L.A."

"You had someone who kept a roof over your head, food on the table. Someone who encouraged you to study."

"Yes, but—" Mitzi's frustration began to churn like an approaching thunderstorm inside her. "I could have gone out and partied. Gotten knocked up at sixteen like my sister."

"You made the most of the opportunities you were given." Keenan's tone seemed to gentle. "That's commendable. I'm not taking anything away from you, Mitzi. I'm simply saying in many ways you were fortunate and had a leg up on a lot of other people. That's all."

Mitzi stared at him for a moment. He made a good point. She hadn't had to take care of her sister, and her mother had done her best to provide for the family.

"You're right." Instead of picking up her pizza, Mitzi stabbed it with her fork. "But I got out of East L.A., left that lifestyle behind because of the choices *I* made."

"Hey." Keenan reached across the table, laid a hand across hers and gave it a squeeze. "You're a success story. You have every right to be proud of what you've achieved."

Some of her irritation slipped away at the admiration in those hazel eyes.

"Care if I join you while I wait for my pizza? I don't want to interrupt."

Jerking back her hand, Mitzi shifted her gaze.

Winston Ferris stood by the table, smiling down at them. From his hand-tailored suit, Hermès tie and black Hublot watch encircling his wrist Winn radiated an aura of wealth and privilege. And why not? He was a successful land developer and son of wealthy rancher Jim Ferris. Though there were some in town who decried his ethics, Mitzi admired his tenacity and focus.

"Please join us." Mitzi moved over and made room for Winn on her side of the booth.

Keenan took another sip of cola and eyed Winn thoughtfully. Once Winn sat down, her dinner companion extended his hand.

"Keenan McGregor," he said. "I don't believe we've met."

Winn introduced himself before Mitzi could do it, then gazed thoughtfully at Keenan. "You're Betsy Harcourt's brother, the one who just got out of prison."

Mitzi's gaze shot to Keenan's face but his expression remained bland.

"That's right," Keenan said easily. "And your father owns the Triple K."

Surprise skittered across Winn's face. "You know my father?"

"I know the spread," Keenan clarified. "I used to do some work for the previous owner back in high school. Prime ranch land."

"Dad is happy with it." Looking perplexed, Winn shifted his attention to Mitzi. "I thought you were dating Kelvin Reid?"

"You're out of the loop, Ferris." Mitzi waved a dismissive hand. "That player is old news."

Winn turned to Keenan, but before he could get a word out, Mitzi continued.

"Keenan and I met at his welcome-home party," she said hurriedly. "Now we're sharing a friendly pizza."

"What she's trying to make clear is this isn't a date." Keenan gave a little chuckle. "I'm not her type. She's not mine."

Mitzi's eyes widened then narrowed. *Not his type.* Whom was he kidding? She'd seen the look in his eyes earlier. If he could have tossed her to the floor and had her right there, he would have.

She ignored the annoying thought that if he had done that,

she'd probably have let him. Of course, desire wasn't the same as being someone's type. Any more than simply sharing a pizza and conversation was a date.

Mitzi watched Keenan stroll out the front door of Perfect Pizza. He'd chatted amiably with Winn but when the man's pizza was delivered and Winn continued to sit, Keenan made some excuse about needing to get home.

She told herself she didn't care if Keenan left. Winn was whom she really wanted to get to know better.

"How's the golf-course development coming?" While Mitzi knew golf was the reason Winn had originally come to Jackson Hole and stayed, those tiny white balls had never been her friend. Whenever she'd had occasion to be around one, it always did everything it could to get away, hiding from her behind rocks, in trees, even plopping deep into water.

"We should be breaking ground soon." Winn leaned back and gazed admiringly across the table at her.

Once Keenan had disappeared from sight, Mitzi suggested Winn move to the other side of the booth so they could face each other. She needed to put a little distance between them. Though his cologne was an expensive brand, she'd never particularly liked the musky scent.

"The environmentally sensitive guidelines have been a thorn in my side," he said, frustration evident in his tone. "Thankfully we're finally in a position to move forward."

"You faced a lot of obstacles," she observed. "But you persevered."

He grinned. "That's the kind of guy I am."

Here, Mitzi thought, was a true kindred spirit. No wonder Winn Ferris currently reigned at the top of her husband list.

As he talked of his boarding school years, his private-school education and his work with GPG, a large investment firm, her mind wandered.

Granted, Winn had achieved much success. He was exactly what she wanted. In fact, he was practically perfect, Mitzi told herself, even as she couldn't help looking at the door and wishing Keenan hadn't hurried off so quickly.

CHAPTER FIVE

"Trust me." Kate passed Mitzi the mashed potatoes at her dinner table the following evening. "You don't want to move into a home that's under construction. It'll be dusty and dirty and dangerous."

"I don't see I have much choice."

"Did I mention *dusty?*"

Mitzi took a small tablespoon of potatoes and passed them to Joel, who so far had wisely kept his mouth shut on the matter.

Mitzi had already discussed the subject with him in depth at the job site today. He'd done his best to change her mind, but she'd dug in her heels. She realized he was frustrated, but in the end, as the client, it was her decision.

"We always have a choice." Kate's gaze shifted from her husband back to her friend, two lines of worry between her brows.

"My swimming teacher didn't give me a choice," ten-year-old Chloe piped up from the other side of Mitzi. "She said I had to tread water for five minutes."

Mitzi smiled sympathetically at the child. "Bummer."

She and Kate had become friends around the time Kate had given birth to Chloe. Mitzi remembered well the pain Kate had experienced when she'd given the baby up for adoption. And she recalled the joy when she'd finally been reunited with her daughter.

Now she and Joel and Chloe were a family. And last year, Samuel Joel Dennes had been born. The energetic boy was currently engrossed with smashing carrots into his high chair tray.

Mitzi turned back to her friend.

"The closing on my condo is at the end of the week," Mitzi reminded her. "Then I'm homeless."

"I made it clear I want you here." Kate's hazel gaze met Mitzi's. "We have a lovely guest room that only gets used when Joel's family comes to visit. Which isn't nearly often enough."

Kate made no mention of her own family, Mitzi knew, because they weren't close. In her parents' minds they had one child, Kate's older sister, Andrea. Though in recent years, Kate and her "perfect sister" had forged a tentative relationship, as far as Mitzi knew, there were no plans for any of Kate's family to visit.

"This is a lovely home," Mitzi said with sincerity, glancing around the room with the large picture window overlooking the mountains. "But I like my privacy."

Kate lifted a brow.

"It's true." Mitzi gave a little laugh. "Blame it on all those years with too many people in a one-bedroom apartment."

"You have a busy practice. Your home should be your sanctuary." Kate reached over and covered Mitzi's hand. "A house still under construction isn't much of a sanctuary. It will be a chaotic place to live."

"Perhaps." Mitzi squeezed Kate's hand then sat back. "I want to give it a try. If it doesn't work, I'll let you say 'I told you so,' and come crawling to your guest room."

"Can't you simply skip the trying-it-out part?" Kate began,

then shook her head at Mitzi's mulish expression. "No, of course you can't."

Kate turned to her husband. She smiled with a confidence nobody at the table believed. "It will be fine. Having Mitzi in the house while you finish the inside won't be a problem. You'll hardly know she's there."

Joel had pulled Keenan off Mitzi's house to work on the house in the mountains. It was for the best. Though Keenan found the woman intriguing, she also irritated the hell out of him.

After a week away, he returned to the house-in-progress and was shocked to discover Mitzi had moved in.

"It's not finished," he said to Bill, incredulous. "Why did Joel allow this?"

A resigned look settled over Bill's wrinkled features. "He didn't allow her anything. She's the client. This is what she wanted."

"What about the dirt? The noise?"

Bill shrugged. "She works long hours. And we've got strict orders to be out of here by five. We've got the doors on, so security shouldn't be a problem. This is a nice neighborhood."

It was the kind of neighborhood Keenan wished he could have given Betsy when she was growing up. Where residents drove slowly because of families riding their bikes, where little girls played dolls on the porches and boys had mock sword fights in the front yard.

Even though he'd started delivering papers at ten, any money he made had gone to help make rent so they had a roof over their heads. That had been the best he could offer his baby sister. Keenan shoved the memories from his mind and concentrated on caulking. Normally, Bill wasn't much of a talker, but today the man was like one of those rabbits with new batteries.

Once his coworker had exhausted every other topic, Bill settled his gaze on Keenan. "What was it you did before being sent to the Big House?"

Keenan didn't take offense. In the short time he'd been working with Bill, his prison stay had quickly become a running joke.

"I was an airplane mechanic." Keenan's voice warmed, the way it always did when he thought about anything to do with flying. "I also had my pilot's license and did some hauling for a charter service."

Clearly perplexed, Bill tilted his head. "Why aren't you doing that now?"

"Couldn't find a job." Keenan shrugged. "Right now, I'm saving up for a deposit on an apartment."

"I thought you were living with your sister."

"Not anymore." Keenan looked down, wiped off some extra caulking with the side of a finger. "She and her husband haven't been married that long. Now with a baby, well, they need their privacy. I got a room downtown."

Betsy, he admitted, had wanted him to stay. She'd actually gotten tears in her eyes when he told her he'd found a room at a boardinghouse. Her husband, Ryan, a buddy from way back, had also tried to convince him to stay, but Keenan refused to be swayed by Betsy's tears or Ryan's logic.

They'd both done so much for him already. Though the room he'd rented was Spartan and the bathroom a shared one down the hall, it was still a step up from a cell.

"You probably need to get some flying time in if you want to get your license back." Bill measured a piece of trim.

"Exactly right." Keenan refused to be discouraged. It might take a few months but he'd fly again. "Time in the air costs money. Once I get an apartment and a few bucks together, that'll be number one on my list."

"My brother, Steve, owns Grand Teton Charter." Bill's gaze

HER KIND OF HERO | 41

fixed on Keenan. "He's been whining about one of his mechanics moving to Colorado. I could hook the two of you up. See if maybe you could do some repair stuff for him in exchange for air time."

Keenan's fingers tightened around the caulking gun. He'd turned down several friends who'd offered to give him money to help him get the air time. This would be bartering services, not charity.

"Sounds like a good plan." Keenan kept his tone casual, not wanting to get his hopes up. Bill's brother might not favor the idea. "Yeah, check and see if he's interested in some kind of arrangement. If not, that's cool."

The rest of the day passed quickly, after Bill promised to speak with Steve that night.

At four-thirty, Bill started gathering up his tools. "My daughter has to work at Hill of Beans this evening and the wife is tied up. I told her I'd get off a little early and take her."

The older man's gaze slid around the room. He grimaced. "I wanted to get the rest of these doors hung today so the painters could start staining tomorrow. Looks like I'm going to have to call and reschedule them."

When the older man pulled out his phone, Keenan held up his hand. "There's only a couple left. I'll stay and finish. There's nowhere I need to be."

"We're supposed to be out of here by five," Bill reminded him.

"You said over lunch you stayed until six last night and Dr. Sanchez still wasn't home," Keenan reminded him.

"That's true." Bill rubbed his chin. "I know she's eager to get this job done. Let's do it this way. You work on it, but if you see her car pull up, you skedaddle out of here. I don't want Joel on my ass."

"Understood." Keenan gave the man a not-so-gentle shove. "Now get out of here. You don't want your daughter to be late."

Keenan continued to work. His radio, set to a hard rock

station, blared out favorite tunes from high school. He'd just finished hanging the last door when the radio cut off.

He looked up.

There she was, dressed in a floaty kind of dress the color of autumn leaves, her hair pulled back in some sort of low twist. Her necklace was copper wire infused with amber and red beads.

Mitzi didn't look angry, he realized. She looked confused.

"What are you doing here?" she asked.

"I could ask you the same thing."

"I live here."

"That's what I heard." He gestured with his head toward the hall leading to the bedroom. "A shower, a bed and a huge mirror. What more does a woman need?"

She gave a throaty laugh. "My sentiments exactly."

He hadn't been sure how she'd respond to seeing him again. It wasn't as if things had gone badly when they'd had dinner. She'd simply found a better-suited dinner companion. He hadn't made a scene, which would have been ridiculous considering the fact they were mere acquaintances.

He glanced at the large sack in her hand, recognized the eatery. "Chinese?"

"I was in the mood." She opened the sack and the delicious aroma of fried rice filled the air. "Golden Palace is the best."

"Got that right," Keenan concurred. He pulled to his feet, dusted his jeans off. "I realize you like us gone by five but if we got all the doors hung today, the painters can come tomorrow and stain."

"Staying late is fine." Mitzi waved a hand and he noticed her nails were the color of pumpkin. "I told Joel I didn't want the workers to feel they had to stay late to try to get the house done sooner, simply because I'd moved in."

"Well, this 'worker' appreciates your consideration."

Mitzi paused for a second then held out the sack, letting it swing as it dangled between her fingers. "If the worker is hungry," she said, "I have enough for two."

"Kind of you to offer." Keenan finished putting away his tools. "I wouldn't want to impose."

"Look, I'm rarely kind. Or thoughtful. And I never let anyone impose. I always order at least enough for two so I have leftovers."

"Nothing like Chinese food for breakfast," he quipped.

"Or cold pizza," she added with an impish smile, and then sighed. "It's been a long day and I'm ready to unwind. I've got a six-pack of imported Chinese beer to go with the food, but there are also bottles of water in the fridge. I'm not in the mood to eat alone, and you're here. The way I see it, unless you have other plans, we might as well eat together."

When she paused to take a breath, Keenan grinned. "Since you put it that way, toss me one of those egg rolls."

After Mitzi changed into jeans and a psychedelic top that Keenan joked made his eyes hurt, they ate sitting crossed-legged on the kitchen floor, the food spread out between them.

He insisted the fried rice and sesame chicken were as good as he remembered, while Mitzi focused on the Mongolian beef and steamed rice. She sipped the cold beer and felt the stress of the day slide away.

She hadn't realized until just this moment that Keenan was really easy to be with, no stress, no pressure. He entertained her with his travels and the life of an extreme-sports junkie. She refrained from bringing up his prison experience.

"I heard you had a place in Teton Village." Keenan dipped his egg roll into some sweet-and-sour sauce. "Minutes from the slopes."

"I take it you like to ski." She took another sip of beer and wondered if there was a single person in Jackson Hole who wasn't crazy about the sport.

He grinned. "I worked on the ski patrol when I was first out of high school."

"What about college?" The question slipped past her lips before she could pull it back.

"No money," he said in a matter-of-fact tone. "No inclination."

He stabbed a bite of sesame chicken with his fork, held it up without eating. "Even if I'd wanted to go, Betsy was still in middle school. And Gloria—our mother—" he clarified at Mitzi's confused look "—you couldn't trust the woman to take care of a dog, much less a child."

Admiration rippled through Mitzi as she put two and two together. Keenan had put his life on hold to watch over his sister.

"Anyway, Bets was the smart one in the family," he continued. "She got a couple of scholarships and some grants and went to the University of Kansas."

"Leaving you finally free to pursue your dreams." Mitzi kept her tone light.

Keenan took the piece of sesame chicken into his mouth, chewed, then swallowed. "My only dreams back then were to have a good time and see how far I could push myself."

She'd known men—boys—like him back in her old neighborhood. They'd lived for today without a thought for their future. She'd avoided them like the plague.

"When did that change?" she asked.

He shot her a lazy glance over the rim of his water bottle. "What makes you think it did?"

"You became an airplane mechanic," she said evenly. "You got your pilot's license."

He leaned back against the wall, his eyes taking on a distant look. "I got tired of all the travel, the different beds, the partying. I didn't want to end up..."

His voice trailed off but Mitzi had no difficulty seeing where

HER KIND OF HERO | 45

he'd been headed. She realized with a start, they weren't so different after all.

"Like your mother," she finished the sentence for him.

He merely shrugged, drank long.

"Things were coming together for me. I even started to think I might one day have enough money together to start my own charter service." He gave a humorless chuckle. "Then it all fell apart."

"What happened?" Even as she asked, Mitzi knew it was none of her business. Realized the topic was probably a difficult one for him to discuss even among friends. While they'd shared a couple of meals, she and Keenan weren't friends, not really.

He could be. Mitzi had the feeling Keenan would make a really good friend.

The day outside was overcast and the room held a soft glow, encouraging confidences. For reasons she chose not to examine too closely, Mitzi wanted to understand the man with the broad shoulders and suddenly tired eyes sitting across from her on the floor.

"I was working late at a private airport outside of Cheyenne." Keenan stared down at the fork in his hand as if he'd never seen the utensil before. "I heard sounds of a scuffle outside the hangar then someone screaming. I ran outside to help."

He hesitated.

Instead of pushing for more, Mitzi took a long, slow sip of her beer and waited.

"Two big guys were pummeling this man who was already down. There was blood. Lots of blood." His eyes grew dark with the memories. "I shouted for them to stop. They stopped all right...and turned on me."

Mitzi's heart caught in her throat. She lowered the glass. "What happened?"

"I got in a couple good jabs." He lifted one shoulder. "Everything after that is a blank. When I woke up I was in an infirmary...attached to the jail."

"You hadn't done anything but try to help."

"I learned I'd been charged with murder. I wasn't worried," he said. "I'd gotten a good look at the two guys and could give their description. Then I discovered the gun that was used to kill the man had been found in my hand."

Mitzi didn't bother to hide her shock. "You were framed."

He nodded. "They did a bang-up job of it. Still, I was prepared to prove my innocence...until I got word if I fought the charges, they'd kill my sister."

Keenan's gaze locked with Mitzi. "I had no doubt they could do it. They knew where Betsy worked, where she lived. I'd have done anything to protect her."

Her gaze didn't waver. "You went to prison for a crime you didn't commit."

"They'd have killed her," he said simply.

"How did you get out?"

"New evidence came to light. Not from me, but from one of the two men there that day. He turned on his friend. Bad guys do things like that. Lucky for me or I'd still be stuck in that hellhole." He gave a humorless chuckle. "Still, it took considerable time, money and effort to secure my release. My sister and my friends here went above and beyond in that area. There's no way I can ever repay them."

Mitzi leaned over, placed her hand over his. "I bet they'd say having you out of prison is all the payment they want."

"Perhaps," he said, not sounding convinced. "Regardless, I'm going to repay every penny they put out. That may take a while. Their kindness, their support, well, that's something I can never repay."

His voice, thick with emotion, cracked, surprising them both.

Keenan attempted to cover the sound with a cough. "Anyway, that's the story. I'm back where I started, and it's okay."

HER KIND OF HERO | 47

"You plan on sticking?"

He nodded. "I want to see my nephew grow up, hang out with friends...although it's different now, most of them being married with kids."

"Tell me about it." Mitzi rolled her eyes. "It's not easy being single and surrounded by happily marrieds."

Keenan's eyes grew sharp, assessing. "I'm surprised someone hasn't snagged you before now."

"Shagged?" She couldn't help but smile. "That's happened a time or two. Or three," she added.

"*Snagged.*" He emphasized the word and laughed. "As in put a ring on that finger."

There were a dozen phrases she'd used over the years to explain her single status, but for some reason Mitzi decided to take the honest route this time.

"For as many years as I can remember, I've had to keep men at arm's length. I had my dreams and nothing—and no one—could be allowed to derail those plans."

"Now you've reached your goal."

"I have," she admitted. "But keeping that distance became a habit. Trust has never come easily for me."

Over fortune cookies, she found herself telling Keenan about Kelvin, her last boyfriend. Although she'd known from the start that the odds of her and the NFL star having a future were a long shot, she'd still been shocked when she learned he'd been cheating on her.

"I let myself trust him," she admitted. "That's where I went totally wrong."

"Did you love him?"

"I was heading in that direction," Mitzi said, embarrassed she could have been so gullible. "I was stupid."

"No," Keenan said firmly. "He was stupid."

Mitzi lifted a shoulder. "My mistake was getting involved with him in the first place. I should have known it wouldn't work. We were apart too much."

"What about Benedict?" Keenan asked.

"Ben's a great guy," she said. "We should have been a perfect match. But he got on my nerves and I got on his. Big-time."

"I can understand that," Keenan said then grinned when she gave him a shove.

"How about you? Any true loves in your past?"

"A prison isn't exactly a dating wonderland." His eyes grew shuttered, the way they always did when those years came up.

Mitzi got it that he didn't want to talk about that time. "I mean before that."

"No. There was never anyone special." His eyes grew thoughtful. "I think I always knew I needed to get myself together before I had anything to offer someone else."

"Any prospects in Jackson Hole?"

"Maybe," he said, a lazy gleam in his eyes.

Her stomach twisted, even as Mitzi told herself it didn't matter to her in the least who Keenan McGregor wanted to date...or to sleep with....

She scrambled to her feet, feeling oddly out of breath. "It's getting late."

Taking his time, Keenan pulled to his feet, hazel eyes focused on hers. "I guess that's my cue to leave."

"It's getting late," she repeated, feeling foolish.

He leaned forward and surprised her by brushing a kiss across her cheek.

Mitzi frowned, resisted the urge to touch her face. "What was that for?"

"For the dinner." He shot her a wink. "Next time, it's my treat."

CHAPTER SIX

"*Next time,* he says, as if it's a given," Mitzi groused to Kate over lunch at the Green Gateau the following day. "He acted as if it was a date or something, and that we were destined to have another one."

"I'll tell Joel he's bothering you." Kate stabbed a crisp piece of endive with her fork.

Mitzi jerked upright. "Don't you dare repeat one word of what I say to your husband."

"If one of his employees is harassing you..." Kate dipped the lettuce into the salad dressing, not seeming to notice Mitzi's horrified expression.

"I didn't say he was harassing me," Mitzi sputtered. "And whatever I tell you is in confidence and not to be shared. I won't have Keenan getting in trouble—"

Suddenly seeing the amusement in her friend's eyes, Mitzi paused. "You had no intention of speaking with Joel."

"Of course not." Kate lifted her hands and drew a box in the air with her fingers. "We're in the vault."

Whatever was said in "the vault" was between the two of them and not to be shared.

"Besides," Kate continued, a tiny smile tugging at her lips, "he's not harassing you—he's flirting."

"You're wrong."

"C'mon, Mitzi, you're not that clueless."

"I've got someone else in mind."

"Tim Duggan?"

Mitzi shook her head. "I thought about it. You were right. I'm not ready to be an instant mommy."

Her expression giving nothing away, Kate took a sip of mango iced tea. "So who's moved to the top of the leader board?"

"Winn Ferris." Mitzi set aside her reservations. Although he didn't make her blood surge like Keenan, there was no denying Winn was an attractive man. And he met all her criteria. "I'm certain the better I get to know him, the more I'll like him."

Kate cocked her head. "Really?"

"Some men have to grow on you."

"Others hit you square in the heart." Kate's lips curved up.

Mitzi felt a stab of envy, knowing her friend was thinking about her reaction to Joel when she'd first met him. Though Kate's journey to love and happiness had been jolted by more than a few potholes, her friend had a marriage Mitzi envied.

But Mitzi had learned long ago that everyone traveled a different course in life. Hers had never been easy. So why should her quest for love and a husband be any different?

"I've got to figure out a way to spend time with Winn." Mitzi caught her lip between her teeth. "I could simply tell him I'm interested, but honesty tends to scare men off."

Kate looked as if she was trying very hard not to laugh. "I agree. Coming out and telling him he's at the top of your husband list might be a trifle disconcerting."

Mitzi shot her friend a glance. "I wish there was a party coming up. A reason to bring us together without being obvious."

"How about book club?"

HER KIND OF HERO | 51

Mitzi had attended the monthly book club in the past when she'd had nothing better to do or was in the mood for gourmet food. It was a given that Lexi Delacourt would supply the entrée consumed prior to the discussion. In addition to being a fine social worker, Lexi was a gourmet cook. Though husbands often showed up with their wives, it wasn't really a party.

"The book club is all women," Mitzi said pointedly. "Winn is a guy."

"During the book club meeting—which happens to be at our house this month—Joel plans to get the guys together for a pickup game of baseball."

A slow smile spread across Mitzi's face. "He could invite Winn."

"He could." Kate handed the waiter her credit card. "I'm sure your Mr. Ferris would attend. Especially considering that many of those who'd be there are the movers and shakers in Jackson Hole, including our new mayor, Tripp Randall."

"Yeah, he'd come." Mitzi brought a finger to her lip. "Unless he has other plans."

"You'll know one way or the other," Kate spoke in a matter-of-fact tone. "You might want to come anyway. Lexi is bringing her fabulous Southern-style fried chicken and we'll be discussing *Catcher in the Rye*, so it should be an enjoyable evening."

"It's next Tuesday, right?" Mitzi scrolled through the calendar in her head.

"Seven o'clock," Kate confirmed.

"I'll be there," Mitzi promised.

This would be a perfect chance to spend some quality time with Winn, perhaps charm him a little. Mitzi wondered why she didn't feel more excited at the prospect.

∾

52 | CINDY KIRK

The second Keenan stepped into the lobby of the Red Sands Hotel, he wondered what madness had prompted him to come. The monthly Jackson After-Hours events gave young professionals in the Jackson Hole area the opportunity to mingle and network.

As Keenan wasn't a professional and at thirty-four didn't feel particularly young, it didn't seem like an event for him. But Gabe and Joel made the event sound mandatory.

Much of the growth Stone Craft Builders had experienced could be traced to contacts made at such events. In Keenan's mind, the only upside was that the complimentary hot hors d'oeuvres would save him from buying or making dinner.

In deference to the event, he'd taken off a half hour early to shower, pull on a pair of khakis and a green polo with the company logo.

When he arrived, the private dining room adjacent to the bar already teemed with people. He recognized many of them, including his brother-in-law.

After getting a glass of club soda from one of the bars, Keenan forced himself to mingle. As he walked through the crowd, he heard a shriek and found himself wrapped in a bear hug.

"Someone told me you were back."

Keenan had a momentary glimpse of bright copper hair tipped with fuchsia and dancing blue eyes framed in purple glasses studded with rhinestones. The girl had blossomed into a woman, but he'd have known that smile anywhere.

"Cassidy Kaye." He returned the hug. "It's been a long time. What are you doing here?"

"Networking," she said and he heard pride in her voice. "I own my own salon...Clippety Do-Dah on Main."

Her gaze narrowed as she studied his hair. "You could use a trim. Stop in and I'll take a few inches off. It'll be like old times, except now I know what I'm doing."

HER KIND OF HERO | 53

"If you need some work done on your car," he said easily, taking a sip of his club soda, "all you had to do was ask."

She chuckled and hugged him again. "You know me so well."

It was the truth. Cassidy had lived down the street from him growing up. All through high school he'd helped keep her ancient Gremlin running. In exchange, she'd cut his hair. Though they never spoke about it, he knew her home life had been no better than his. But she was tough and from all appearances had come out ahead.

She scanned the crowd, her lips lifting in a rueful smile. "Ever think you and me'd be standing here mingling with Jackson's elite?"

"Oh, yeah," he drawled. "All I had to do was get out of prison first."

She laughed.

He narrowed his gaze. "Is that Doogie over there?"

Cassidy smiled. "That's him."

Dr. Timothy Duggan had been another classmate Keenan had lost track of over the years. From the time he'd been a small child, the awkward red-haired kid had wanted to be a doctor. That fact, coupled with old reruns of *Doogie Howser, MD* and a last name of Duggan, had sealed Tim's fate. He'd been dubbed Doogie in middle school. The name had stuck.

While Keenan and Cassidy had been from the wrong side of the tracks, Tim had come from a wealthy family. Still, he'd been a good guy and had once been a friend.

Keenan noted Tim's red hair had darkened over time and was now the color of mahogany.

"I haven't seen him since high school," he told Cass.

Even as the thought of walking over and greeting his old friend crossed his mind, Winn Ferris and Mitzi paused to speak with Tim.

Cassidy's expression narrowed. "That's Winn Ferris and Mit—"

"I know the other two." A hard knot had formed in the pit of Keenan's stomach.

Keenan felt Cassidy's curious gaze at the curtness in his tone.

"Let's go say hello."

Before he could respond, she had her hand on his arm and was tugging him across the room.

Mitzi told herself the evening was moving along splendidly. She already planned to see Winn at the upcoming book club meeting, so running into him tonight was an extra bonus. She barely had time to get a glass of wine when he'd sought her out.

The gold cashmere dress and heels had earned Winn's effusive praise. He also liked her hair, which tonight was a subdued brown with blond highlights.

She thought hair color should have more pop, like Cassidy Kaye's hot pink tips. Like Cassidy, Mitzi shared a love of changing hair colors as often as other women changed shoes or men. But she couldn't go wild and crazy like Cass. Common sense told her patients wouldn't accept a pink-haired orthopedic surgeon.

Tonight Cassidy had brought a date. Mitzi's lips curved before her smile froze.

Her heart gave a little jolt at the sight of Keenan. Though his attire for the evening fell squarely into the business casual arena, he looked good enough to eat.

She pulled her attention from him and listened to Winn discuss—again—the golf development planned for Jackson Hole with Tim. It was good, she told herself, that he was so passionate about the project.

Perhaps it was her background, but she found it difficult to get excited about a sport that wasted so much of a person's time and money. Still, she plastered an interested expression on her

HER KIND OF HERO | 55

face, even as she wondered if she should place Tim Duggan back on her husband list.

Though he listened respectfully as Winn droned on, she could see him looking for an escape route. Despite being a father of two, Tim was attractive, in a boyishly handsome way. Still, two kids was a definite negative.

"Hey, guys. Are you talking about how hot I look this evening?"

Mitzi turned toward the sassy feminine voice, along with Winn and Tim.

"We don't mean to interrupt," Keenan said firmly.

We.

Mitzi's smile froze on her lips. Had Keenan come to the party with Cassidy?

"Keenan was just saying that he hadn't touched base with you since he was back, Dr. Duggan." Cassidy's voice picked up speed and red splotches appeared on her neck. "So I dragged him over here."

"*Doctor* Duggan?" Keenan rolled his eyes. "Sheesh, Cass. We went to school with Doogie."

"Doogie?" Mitzi raised a brow.

Tim met Keenan's eyes. "I'm not into violence, Keenan. But if you call me that again, I may have to punch you."

Though there was a definite warning in the tone, Mitzi detected true affection between the two men.

"Boys, boys." Cassidy stepped between them then focused on Tim. "You didn't mean to upset *Doogie,* did you, Keenan?"

Before Keenan could respond, Cassidy placed a hand to her mouth and shot Tim an impish smile. "Oops, that just slipped out. Are you going to punch me, too?"

Tim laughed.

"It's great to see you, Cassidy," he said easily, then held out his hand to Keenan. "It's been a long time. I was sorry I couldn't make your welcome-home party. One of my girls was sick."

Mitzi watched the interaction between Keenan and Tim. There was an ease between the two men that hadn't been present when Tim and Winn had been discussing business. Of course, Keenan and Tim had grown up in Jackson Hole. Like her, Winn was an outsider.

She pulled her attention to Cassidy. "I love your hair."

A quick smile told Mitzi the compliment was appreciated.

"Thanks. I like how you shake things up all the time with yours." Cassidy's gaze lingered, turned assessing. "Tonight it's a little more...subdued."

Though it was clear Cassidy didn't approve of her hairstyle tonight, Mitzi didn't take offense. Kate had often told Mitzi she was like a chameleon, changing her look depending on the circumstances. All true. "I thought it was appropriate for the crowd."

"Coward," Cassidy retorted and made Mitzi laugh.

"Did you and Keenan come together?" Mitzi asked casually in a low tone.

Cassidy heaved a heartfelt sigh. "I wish."

"Oh—"

"It's not happening," Cassidy added with an even heavier sigh. "Too much history, too many years, never got together, never will. Besides..."

The hairstylist crooked a gold-tipped nail and motioned Mitzi close.

Mitzi took a sip of champagne, leaned close.

"The man's only got eyes for you."

Mitzi inhaled sharply then began to cough. She quickly brought herself under control.

Cassidy's eyes danced with good humor as Mitzi's gaze slipped to Keenan. He appeared so relaxed, laughing with Tim over some incident that had happened years ago on the football field.

HER KIND OF HERO | 57

Determinedly she shifted her gaze to Winn, who stood with a mildly bored expression sipping a glass of wine.

She thought about engaging him in conversation but feared if he brought up the golf-course development again, she might snap. Besides, it had been her surgery day and she was exhausted.

The book club event at Kate's home on Tuesday would be soon enough to get to know Winn Ferris better.

CHAPTER SEVEN

Keenan thought about skipping the baseball game. But it had been a long time since he'd played with friends. He'd played ball in high school and loved it. And he was good. Not as good as he'd been at football, where his prowess had earned him a scholarship. That was in the past. Tonight Joel had sweetened the invitation by promising dinner.

He took a quick shower after work then pulled on a clean pair of jeans and a white T-shirt. Many of Keenan's old friends were planning to attend while their wives met for a monthly book club. He pulled into the long drive leading up to the large stone and log home in the mountains and found himself wishing Mitzi would be here.

When he'd casually asked Joel who usually showed up for these types of events, the list of people he rattled off didn't include her.

All the better. His attraction to Mitzi was a dead-end road. While he enjoyed her company, she obviously had her sights set on Winn Ferris.

Though Winn came off as intense, something told Keenan there was a good guy beneath those hand-tailored suits and

HER KIND OF HERO | 59

Italian shoes. He reminded Keenan a little bit of himself in high school when he'd put on a front, acting as if acceptance didn't matter when it mattered very much.

Keenan wasn't going to let the fact that Mitzi was attracted to the executive bring his spirits down. Not tonight. Not when he'd gotten such good news earlier. Bill's brother *was* interested in bartering mechanic services for air time.

Tomorrow, he'd be able to fly for the first time in nearly three years. He couldn't wait.

Keenan parked his early eighties Impala in the drive behind a cherry-red BMW then strode to the front door. Pleasure surged through his veins. Things were looking up.

Joel opened the door and Keenan was greeted by an explosion of noise. His boss had warned him that everyone would bring their children, but he hadn't expected there to be so many of them.

"We've got a couple of sitters who'll be watching the children," Joel assured him. "Though we might enlist some of the older kids to stand in the outfield and shag stray balls."

Keenan had to jump back to avoid colliding with a pair of curly-haired twin boys racing past him.

"Walk," Joel ordered.

The two immediately slowed to a walk for a second, then sped up again before they reached the next room.

Joel shook his head. "Those two are Travis Fisher's oldest set of twins. The man deserves combat pay."

"Oldest set?" Keenan asked.

"He and MK have got another boy, then a set of boy-girl twins."

Keenan thought back. The oldest of seven—or was it eight?—Travis had been very vocal about remaining childless. "Travis always said he didn't want any kids."

"He changed his mind," Joel said with a laugh, then directed Keenan's attention to a large table in the great room covered by a red-and-white checkered tablecloth. "Kate decided to serve buffet-style tonight."

The Western theme was carried on in the small oil lanterns in various colors on the table, copper vases filled with sunflowers and silverware wrapped in bandanas of red and blue. Large crockery bowls filled with salads and vegetables dotted the top of the table, with a basket of assorted rolls at one end. His gaze settled on the towering platters of crisp fried chicken, and Keenan's mouth watered.

When Joel mentioned Lexi would be catering and added that she was a gourmet cook, Keenan had worried the food would be fancy stuff with edible flowers. Instead there was fried chicken and potato salad. Both personal favorites.

The doorbell rang. Joel slapped his back. "Make yourself at home."

Keenan meandered around the room for a minute then stopped short. A prickle of awareness traveled up his spine. He turned and there she was, wearing a turquoise skirt and a white filmy blouse scooped low in the front. Heeled boots with strips of turquoise showed off slim calves. Tousled brown hair streaked with gold was pulled back from her face in a shiny silver clip.

He told himself to look away, to not be so obvious, but he couldn't pull his gaze from Mitzi. Keenan couldn't believe she was here. A book club hardly seemed her style.

Then again, it was a party, and that was definitely her style.

He started across the room then stopped when Joel ushered in the latest arrival. Keenan frowned. Was that why Mitzi had come? To see Winn Ferris?

Whom the doctor socialized with was none of his business. Still, like a bright light fading to black, his pleasure in the evening dimmed considerably.

"I bet you don't remember me."

Keenan turned to find an attractive blonde with big blue eyes

HER KIND OF HERO | 61

smiling up at him. She was petite but, based on her jean skirt and form-fitting top, curvy in all the right places.

He pulled his brows together, searched his memory banks but came up empty. "Give me a hint."

She extended her hand with pink-tipped nails. "Hailey Randall."

Recognition flooded him. "That's right. Tripp's little sister."

Hailey visibly winced. "I really wish everyone wouldn't say that."

"Hey, to most people, I'm Betsy's big brother."

Hailey tilted her head, considered him. "You're sweet." She looped her arm through his. "You can buy me a drink."

"They're charging for drinks?"

She laughed, a silver tinkle. "Let me rephrase. You can get me a drink."

"It would be my pleasure." As they made their way to the bar in one corner, Keenan tried to recall what he knew about Tripp's little sister. If he was remembering correctly, she'd been in his sister Betsy's grade.

She'd been a chatterbox, a pigtailed dynamo who'd tagged along behind Tripp every chance she got and tattled whenever her brother even *thought* about doing anything wrong.

Hailey had been a child the last time he'd seen her, but the woman at his side had definitely grown up.

"Tell me what you've been doing," he said conversationally as they waited for the waiter to pour her a glass of wine and refill his club soda. "Last time I saw you I believe you were in middle school and had braces."

"Keenan," she teased, rolling her eyes. "You're not supposed to say stuff like that to a woman."

"You're not a woman," he said deadpan. "You're Tripp's—"

"—little sister." She heaved a melodramatic sigh. "Yes, I know. But just for tonight, could you please forget that fact?"

"Your wish is my command."

It was corny but it made her giggle. Resisting the urge to glance in the direction he'd last seen Mitzi, Keenan focused on the woman at his side and gave her his total attention. "C'mon, Hailey. Tell Betsy's big brother what you've been doing since middle—ah—since the last I saw you."

~

Mitzi watched Keenan and Hailey from across the room. The couple was laughing and appeared to be having a good time.

"I didn't realize they were such good friends."

Mitzi turned. Winn stood beside her, the stem of a wineglass clamped tightly between his fingers.

"I'm not sure they are."

"Looks that way to me," he muttered.

Mitzi hadn't spent much time with Hailey, and what she recalled about the young woman could fit into a teaspoon. She knew Hailey was a speech therapist who'd returned to Jackson Hole when her father's health had been tenuous. According to the gossip, Frank Randall had responded well to a change in chemotherapy and was now in full remission.

Hailey wasn't yet working full-time but was helping out at her parents' ranch and working PRN—as needed—as a speech therapist at the hospital. The girl was bright, bubbly and always seemed to have a smile on her face. Mitzi could see why she'd caught Keenan's eye. And judging by the look on Winn's face, his, as well.

"Let's go say hello." Winn grabbed her arm and practically pulled her across the room.

Mitzi plastered a smile on her face.

Winn slowed his steps to a saunter as they closed in on the couple. They reached them just as Joel called out for everyone to get some food and grab a seat. According to the evening's schedule of events, they had a mere thirty minutes to eat before the book club started inside and the first pitch was thrown outside.

A small table for four with a red tablecloth was open next to where they stood.

Hailey smiled at Winn and Mitzi, and gestured with one hand. "We could all sit here? Unless you've already gotten a space elsewhere?"

"Thanks, Hailey. This works for me." She glanced at Winn. "Okay with you?"

Somehow, in the buffet line, Keenan ended up behind her.

"You don't seem the book-club type to me," Keenan murmured. "No disrespect intended."

Mitzi laughed, inhaling the faintly intoxicating scent of his scent, a delicious blend of soap, wood and red-blooded male. "I'm not."

"Why are you here?"

She shrugged. "Kate's my dearest friend. You?"

Keenan's lips quirked upward. "Joel's my boss."

"You win." She laughed. "Your reason is more compelling."

"What book are you discussing tonight?"

She slanted him a sidelong glance. "Is that a trick question?"

"I thought that's what was happening after dinner."

Mitzi pursed her lips. "Kate may have mentioned some book."

"You didn't read it?"

"I was supposed to read it?" Mitzi lowered her voice. "I shouldn't probably admit this, but I'm not much of a reader."

"I'm not, either," he said easily, reaching around her to grab two plates, then handing one to her. "I pretended to love it when Betsy was little, because I knew it was important. She loves to read."

"You were a good big brother."

"I tried," he said, his eyes taking on a distant look. "I could have done better."

Mitzi didn't want to look back too far or think of her own

sister. Perhaps she could have helped her. Perhaps not. Growing up, it had been every sister for herself. Which now seemed a bit sad. "I'm a firm believer in leaving the past in the past."

"You're right." He grabbed two rolls and tossed one on her plate and the other on his. "Looking ahead holds so much more appeal. Take you, for example. Soon you'll have a brand-new house and no workmen underfoot."

"I am looking forward to it being done." Mitzi hadn't realized how much she counted on her home being her sanctuary until she'd moved into chaos instead of solitude. "What are you looking forward to?"

"Getting my pilot's license back." Keenan heaped some potato salad on a plate. "I have my aviation physical scheduled for Friday. A guy I work with, his brother is a flight instructor. He's taking me up so I can sharpen my rusty skills and get some hours in the air. Then I should be all set."

"After you get your license, then what?" Mitzi took a spoonful of pasta salad. "I mean, it's not like you have access to a plane or anything."

His mouth tightened as he focused on the plethora of salads and side dishes spread out before him.

"I'm sorry," she said quickly, placing a hand on his arm.

"No reason to apologize. You only spoke the truth," he said evenly.

"Knowing you, you'll find a way to get in the air."

"I think I may have already found it. Until it's all settled, I'm not counting on anything."

After spending so much time behind bars, he deserved some good luck. If she'd been in his situation, she'd have been bitter. From what she'd observed so far, he'd simply moved on. "What kind of way have you found?"

"You know Bill—" Keenan began, waited for Mitzi's nod. "His brother, Steve, said I can use his plane in exchange for mechanic work."

HER KIND OF HERO | 65

"Steve?" Mitzi paused as the name settled over her. "What's his last name?"

"Kowalski." Keenan glanced at her. "Do you know him?"

Mitzi nodded. "Ben uses one of his planes to fly to the rural clinics the practice does across the state."

"No kidding. How often are these clinics?"

"It varies depending on how many patients are scheduled. At least once a month, sometimes more often."

"Move it along." Hailey tapped Mitzi on the shoulder. "Quit with the conversation."

Mitzi glanced around and realized with sudden horror that she'd gotten so engrossed talking with Keenan that she'd stopped walking and was holding up the line.

She made quick work of filling her plate then forced her attention to Winn once they were all seated. It wouldn't do for him to get the idea she was interested in a romantic relationship with Keenan.

Hailey and Winn had apparently been discussing tonight's book club selection—*Catcher in the Rye*—and continued the discussion once seated.

"What did you think of the protagonist?" Hailey asked Mitzi. "Did you find him overly judgmental?"

Mitzi could spout nonsense with the best of them, but she was tired and for once honesty seemed the best policy. "I know I read the book. Or I think I read it. After all, it's a classic. All I can remember right now is that the narrator had a funky name."

"Holden Caulfield," Hailey said and Winn smiled.

"That's more than I remember," Keenan said, not appearing the least embarrassed by the admission.

"Winn and I both love the book," Hailey said with way too much enthusiasm. "I told him it was too bad he has to play baseball. He has such great insight on several aspects of the novel."

"We could switch," Mitzi offered, only half joking. "Except I'm not into baseball, either."

Hailey cocked her head. "What is it you like to do, Mitzi?"

The woman sounded as if she was genuinely interested. But Mitzi knew her answer would make her sound superficial rather than scholarly.

If the shoe fit...

"I like to shop," Mitzi admitted. "I like to travel, see new places. I like to decorate my home."

"I like to shop, too." Hailey flashed a bright smile in Mitzi's direction. "Anytime you need a shopping buddy, give me a call."

"I will," Mitzi said, finding it impossible not to like her.

Mitzi found herself paying more attention to her conversation with Hailey than she did to the plate in front of her. So when Kate announced it was time for the book-club discussion to begin and Joel started gathering up the players for the baseball game, her plate had barely been touched.

"I'll join you in the family room in a minute," she told Kate. "I skipped lunch, so I'm going to finish eating first."

"Bring your plate with you," Kate offered. "Eat while we discuss."

To Mitzi's way of thinking, that would be the quickest way to ruin an appetite.

"Start without me." Mitzi waved a hand in the air. "I'll be in soon."

Winn and Hailey had already left the table, but Keenan remained seated. She heard him tell Joel not to wait on him.

"Go outside," she told him.

"I'm in no rush, either." Keenan studied her thoughtfully. "In fact, I wouldn't mind us cutting out and finding our own entertainment. What do you say, Mitzi? Want to play hooky with me?"

CHAPTER EIGHT

Keenan couldn't believe he expected Mitzi to leave her friend's party. But when she tilted her head and the air surrounding them began to sizzle, the impulsive gesture made sense.

He wanted her. With him. Alone.

The thought was so far from baseball and book clubs that he had to grin.

A spark of interest flared in her blue eyes. "What do you have in mind?"

You. Me. Naked.

"I'm open to just about anything." The fact that she asked told Keenan she was halfway out the door with him already. "The only thing off-limits is any discussion of *Catcher in the Rye.*"

Mitzi took a sip of wine. Considered.

Keenan reined in impatience. Was Winn the reason she was hesitating? Or did she simply want to hang with her friends this evening? God, he hoped not.

"Forget it." Keenan swiped the air with his hand in a careless gesture. "You're here because of the book club—"

"Can you really believe I want to spend the rest of my evening discussing some horrid story that I haven't even read?" She curved her fingers around his biceps, and those luscious red-painted lips curved in a sly smile. "It'll be like a jailbreak."

Glancing around the warm and homey interior, at the table with its mountain of food, Keenan thought of the cell that had been his home in the Rawlins penitentiary. Jail? Not hardly. Still, he'd play along.

"Do you have a hideout in mind if Joel and Kate turn the dogs loose?"

Mitzi's smile widened. "Of course I do."

"Where?"

"You'll see."

Though it would have been Keenan's preference to slip out unnoticed, good manners dictated otherwise. Mitzi strolled into the family room to tell Kate, while he pulled Joel aside outside. Then they were free, and the winding road down the mountain beckoned.

Mitzi's snazzy sports car zipped around curves then picked up even more speed on the highway into Jackson. She said she'd lead the way and he promised to follow. He didn't expect the abrupt turn into the parking lot of a big-box store on the edge of town.

He wheeled his clunker next to her sporty BMW and got out. "Remembered some last-minute shopping?"

"In a manner of speaking." Without looking to see if he would follow, she began walking toward the front of the store. "Tonight is Tuesday."

He hurried to catch up. "Thanks for the news bulletin."

The automatic doors slid open. The metal beams and fluorescent lights reminded him of a similar place that had been his second home growing up. That store had everything an impoverished family needed, including air-conditioning during the hottest summer days.

"It's sample night." Mitzi tossed her head, sending her glorious mane of hair scattering around her shoulders like falling autumn leaves. "Every Tuesday they set up food stations in the grocery section. You can eat for free."

She was serious in her glee, and a spark of anticipation made her blue eyes shine.

Her enthusiasm made Keenan smile. "How do you know stuff like this?"

"I spent my share of years living on little to no money. I consider myself an expert on finding ways to conserve." Mitzi smiled at the woman in the bright red smock and continued with purposeful steps past the customer service center to the grocery section. "They have this once a week. Every Tuesday. Until you get on your feet, you might want to keep it in mind."

Until you get on your feet.

She understood—no *believed*—he wouldn't be living paycheck to paycheck forever.

"I knew this night was on an upswing." Her eyes lit up at the sight of the first sample station. "Shrimp. Yum." For a second, he thought about mentioning the fried chicken and all the fabulous side dishes at Joel and Kate's. But then he realized this wasn't about food. It was about adventure, doing the unexpected and helping out a friend.

"I'd like a sample, please." Mitzi flashed the older woman with the tightly permed gray hair a bright smile then accepted a small plastic cup holding three boiled shrimp.

Keenan waited.

Mitzi gestured with her head toward him. "My friend, he'd like a sample, too."

Her friend. It had a good sound.

Keenan held out a hand for the shrimp.

Mitzi enjoyed the hour she spent with Keenan wandering up and down the aisles, sampling everything from black-bean chips to tiny bites of cake. The only item she refused was the chewy coconut macaroons.

70 | CINDY KIRK

"I hate anything with coconut," she confided to Keenan, even as he eagerly reached for the sample.

So far she'd enjoyed the outing. With Keenan, she could be herself. Mitzi liked exchanging stories from childhood. Stories that others would find difficult to comprehend or perhaps even think she was joking.

She told him about studying every evening in the dilapidated library near her home because the place had air-conditioning and an internet connection. He confided spending time at home, even when he would have preferred to be running with his school-mates, because he didn't trust his mother's "friends" around Betsy.

Because Mitzi wasn't interested in Keenan romantically, it was easy to be honest. Once they'd visited the last sample station, they stepped out into the Indian-summer-night air. Being on the edge of Jackson was almost like being in the country.

Mitzi paused to gaze into the clear, star-filled sky. Keenan stood beside her, his head cocked back, his eyes focused up.

She briefly considered taking his hand...just because...but instead fell into step beside him.

It was warm for September, which was why most of the women shoppers they passed wore shorts or capris and sandals. Mitzi felt a bit overdressed in her flowing skirt, blousy top and heeled boots. But if the admiring glances sent her way were any indication, most men—including Keenan—liked what she wore.

"Did I mention I'm going to be flying to—" She gaped as Keenan took off running across the asphalt lot.

Mitzi watched first in irritated puzzlement then in horror as he headed directly into the path of a mammoth four-by-four.

"Keenan." His name ripped from her throat, though she doubted he heard her over the truck's pounding bass.

The driver missed him by inches, flipped up his middle finger, then hit the gas and sped from the lot.

Mitzi raced across the asphalt lot, her heart pounding. She

slid to a stop in front of him, grabbed his arm in a death grip. "Are you crazy? You could have been killed. Whatever made you—"

Then she saw it. A tiny gray kitten cradled in his large, callused hands. While Mitzi stared, the animal lifted its head, fixed its green eyes on her and mewed.

The fur was longish but couldn't hide that the kitten was beyond skinny. Ribs were prominent and green eyes enormous in a too-thin face.

Keenan's eyes met hers. "He'd have run over her." His voice held an icy edge. "He saw her and could have easily missed her. But he wanted to hit her."

He stared into the distance, his eyes as cold as his words.

"Bastard," he spat.

Mitzi turned in time to see the lights of the truck disappear from view.

"I've known men like him." She thought of her sister's second husband and shivered. "Guys into hurting women, children, animals, just because they can."

A plaintive mew pulled Mitzi's attention back to Keenan.

She stepped close, stroked the kitten's head with two gentle fingers. "She's tiny. How old do you think she is?"

Keenan pulled his gaze from the darkness. His eyes softened. "I'm guessing about four weeks."

"What are we going to do with her?" Mitzi glanced around the parking lot, at all the cars and trucks entering and exiting. For a baby like this one, danger was everywhere. She pulled her brows together in a worried frown. "We can't leave her here."

"No," he agreed. "She'll be hit. Or wander from the parking lot into the darkness and an animal will get her. We'll drop her off at the shelter. She'll be safe there."

Mitzi started to shake her head even before he finished speaking. "According to the local news the shelter already has too many cats. Next weekend they're offering special pricing to try to reduce the number."

"It's not fair," Keenan murmured almost to himself. "Her life has barely begun and already she struggles."

"You could keep her," Mitzi suggested hopefully as they slowly crossed the lot to their vehicles.

"Can't." The word hung heavy with regret. "The boarding-house where I live doesn't allow pets."

"What about your sister?"

"Puffy, their Pomeranian, despises cats." Keenan paused when they reached her BMW. His hazel eyes met hers, held. "You could take her."

"Me?" Surprise had the word coming out on a squeak.

"You have a house."

"A house under construction," she reminded him. Still, her gaze was drawn now to the kitten resting contentedly in the crook of his arm.

"Cats don't need a lot of care." Keenan rested a hand on the top of the low-slung car. "You had one. You know."

Oreo. Mitzi's heart lurched. The black-and-white had been one of the true bright lights of her childhood.

"Cats are self-sufficient." Keenan's tone turned persuasive. "Give 'em a litter box, food and water, and they're happy."

Mitzi gazed down at the kitten. "I wonder if I could teach her to do tricks like you did with Mr. Tubs."

"You'll keep her?" Relief etched itself on his face and sounded in his voice.

"I don't see I have much choice." Mitzi scooped the kitty from his arms, held her close then smiled as the animal began to purr. "She needed a break. Tonight she gets two. You saved her life. I'll give her a home."

∿

HER KIND OF HERO | 73

The next couple of days passed quickly. Keenan saw the kitten, but not Mitzi. On Thursday, when he packed up his tools and headed to his car, she still wasn't home.

He fought a surge of disappointment. It wasn't that he was desperate to see her, he was merely curious how she and the kitten were getting along. All afternoon he'd had the feeling this was the day their paths would cross again. But he couldn't hang around and wait any longer. Keenan had discovered Ben Campbell was an aviation medical examiner.

He'd been able to secure a late-afternoon appointment, scheduled after the doctor saw his last patient. He arrived a few minutes early, eager to complete the first step toward getting his pilot's license.

Spring Gulch Orthopedics was an impressive structure, brick edged with stone with a massive timbered entry. As Keenan walked through the heavy wooden front doors with edged glass, it struck him how far apart his world was from the one Mitzi now inhabited.

They may have started out in similar situations but they were in far different places now. Not that it mattered. They were simply friends.

After checking in, Keenan took a seat in the waiting area and picked up a magazine.

"Mr. McGregor." The receptionist, a cool and composed woman, with streaks of gray in her brown hair and steely blue eyes, motioned to him. "Dr. Campbell can see you now."

As expected, the exam was over quickly. Afterward he and Ben talked for several minutes, catching up. The doctor mentioned he'd married one of Keenan's classmates and they'd recently had a son.

"Because of my family, I like to stick close to home," Ben confided as they strolled to the lobby. "I used to fly myself to the rural clinics, which was a good opportunity to get in some air time. Going forward, Dr. Sanchez will be making those trips.

74 | CINDY KIRK

We've contracted with Grand Teton to provide the plane and the pilot."

Keenan's ear perked up. Grand Teton was the firm Bill's brother, Steve Kowalski, owned. Keenan had high hopes that once he got his license, Steve would hire him to fill in as needed.

"Ben, are you busy?"

From the back of the medical office building, a feminine voice called out.

Keenan recognized the sultry lilt immediately. His heart lurched. *Mitzi.*

"In the lobby," Ben said.

"I stopped in to see Mrs. Roth while I was at the hospital and—"

Surprise skittered across Mitzi's face. She wore a white lab coat over a dress of vivid blue. Her hair was pulled back in some kind of twist. While her heels were incredibly sexy, simply looking at the high arch made Keenan's feet ache. A stethoscope peeked out from one pocket. "Keenan. What are you doing here?"

Before he could respond, she flushed. "I'm sorry. Not my business."

Ben's gaze shifted from Mitzi to Keenan. "You two know each other?"

"I work for Joel Dennes," Keenan spoke easily. "His company is building Dr. Sanchez's new home."

Puzzlement filled Mitzi's eyes. He could see her trying to decide if he was simply answering the question or deliberately distancing himself from her.

"I've been pleased with the results." Mitzi's gaze shifted from Keenan's legs to his arms. Worry filled her eyes and the look of puzzlement returned. "Okay, it's not my business, but...did you injure yourself?"

"Nothing that exciting." Keenan chuckled. "Aviation exam."

"Oh. Good." She expelled a breath, her fingers fluttering to her hair.

HER KIND OF HERO | 75

"I need to run." Ben extended his hand. "It was great seeing you again, Keenan."

Ben turned to Mitzi. "Mrs. Roth?"

"Nothing urgent. I can update you in the morning."

"Sounds good." Ben glanced at the door. "You're the last one here."

"I'll lock up," she told him.

When Keenan started to walk out after Ben, Mitzi grabbed his arm. "May I speak with you a minute?"

"Sure."

Silence descended as the door clicked shut. The past few days Keenan had found himself hoping their paths would cross. He'd missed seeing her, talking to her, laughing with her. Now, she stood less than a foot away and he was as tongue-tied as a sixteen-year-old.

Mitzi cleared her throat. He wasn't the only one having difficulty finding a voice. "I want to thank you for watching out for Itty Bitty."

Keenan grimaced. "That's what you decided to call her?"

He conveniently disregarded the fact that he and Bill had taken to calling the gray puff of fur "Miss Kitty," which wasn't much better.

Mitzi looked amused. "You don't approve?"

"Seems a little...lame."

"This from a man who had a cat named Mr. Tubs?"

"I was a kid when I came up with that name." Then he thought of "Miss Kitty" and surrendered. "Itty Bitty is as good of a name as any. And there's no need to thank me since I haven't done anything."

"I beg to differ." She took a step closer and a familiar sizzle sparked in his belly. "When I get home, her litter box has been cleaned and she has fresh water. She's smart but I doubt she's handling those tasks herself."

He simply grinned.

"Well." She expelled a breath. "Thank you."

Keenan jammed his hands into his pockets. "Are you happy you kept her?"

He prayed she'd say yes. He wasn't sure where he'd start if he had to search for a new home. Keenan hadn't been lying when he'd told her neither he nor his sister could take the kitten. But he wouldn't let Miss Kitty, er, Itty Bitty, become one of many at an overcrowded shelter.

Mitzi's eyes warmed. "I like having her waiting for me at the end of the day."

"You work long hours."

"Tell me about it." She raked a hand through her hair, and he saw weariness edging those beautiful blue eyes.

"It's important to have balance."

"You're preaching to the choir. It's just that lately I haven't been able to fit in the fun."

Not a problem. When an idea popped into his head, he smiled. He'd always been a master at seizing the moment. "Ever windsurfed?"

Mitzi shook her head. "Never tried it."

"Jackson Lake is close." Keenan kept his tone offhand. "There's enough daylight left for me to give you a brief introduction to the sport. You'll love it."

"It's warm outside," she said slowly, as if genuinely considering the invitation. "But won't the water be cold?"

"That's what wetsuits are for." Keenan smiled winningly. "C'mon, Mitzi, you know you want to do it."

"You're right. It sounds like great fun." Mitzi looped her arm through his and grinned. "And just what this doctor needs after a long day."

∽

Mitzi fought to the water's surface and gulped air. Though windsurfing might look easy, sound easy, she'd discovered the sport was darn hard. Even for someone in good shape.

She worked out regularly. Not only because she liked having a tight and toned body but because endurance was essential for long surgeries. Her tight core made standing on the board and finding her balance easy. Pulling the sail out of the water using the uphaul proved more...difficult. Maneuvering that sail to capture the wind while keeping her balance demanded concentration and skill.

"Weight in harness, front foot in." She repeated the mantra to herself during what she suspected would be her final chance.

This last time, she'd gotten it right. The board had skimmed the water until she'd gotten close to shore and gone over. A keen sense of accomplishment mixed with exhilaration.

Keenan appeared beside her, treading water, a grin on her lips. "You looked like a pro out there."

Though his words pleased her, *pro* was stretching it...by a mile.

"You're the one who's good. I'm guessing you've done this a few times."

"Let's just say that fun—" he shot her a wink "—used to be my life."

Mitzi rested her hand on the floating board. "I want to do it again."

"Another time." He swam closer. "It's getting dark. We'll take a breather then haul these out."

"I don't need a breath—"

"Hands on my shoulders," he ordered.

Shocked at the command in his tone, she obeyed.

"Wrap your legs around my waist."

When she did, Keenan leaned back slightly and floated, easily holding them both up.

His water-slicked suit was hot, warmed by the once-bright

sun. Mahogany hair glistened in the light. Hazel eyes, fringed with dark lashes, met hers.

Mitzi's heart thumped noisily against her ribs. The familiar pull had her bringing fingers to the silky hair at the nape of his neck.

"This is fun, too," she murmured.

He watched her speculatively for a moment. "I hope you like this, too."

Keenan leaned in and pressed warm lips against hers. Though the kiss was light and sweet, it made her tremble.

"We shouldn't do this," she said.

"Why not?" If he had any doubts, it didn't show. There was a spark of mischief in his hazel eyes. "We're friends. Friends kiss."

He was right, of course. There was no need to make such a big deal out of something as innocuous as two mouths coming together.

She twined her fingers in his hair, desire curling in her belly. "You know how some people can stop at just one potato chip?"

He cocked his head, his gaze quizzical.

"I've never been that kind of gal," she said and closed her mouth over his for one more kiss.

CHAPTER NINE

It was almost one by the time Keenan settled under a large shade tree in Mitzi's lawn to eat his lunch. He opened the brown bag just as a car pulled into the driveway. By the time his sister got out and unstrapped his nephew from his safety seat, he'd reached the vehicle.

Nate squealed when he saw him, his mouth open in a wide baby smile as his chubby legs chewed up the short distance between them.

In one fluid movement, Keenan scooped the child up and swung him around.

"Not too high," Betsy warned. "He ate less than an hour ago."

Sufficiently warned, Keenan settled for placing the boy on his shoulders. He shifted his gaze to his sister. In her gold jeans and multicolored shirt, Betsy reminded him of a stylish butterfly.

But it was the look of contentment in her eyes that had his heart stuttering with relief. After everything she'd been through, Betsy was happy.

He took the oversize bag from her shoulder and motioned her into the shade of the oak tree he'd been sitting under only moments before. Though it wasn't particularly hot for

September, the sun was high and bright in the cloudless sky. "What brings you out this way?"

Though many of their friends lived close, Betsy and Ryan lived in Jackson. She'd inherited their Aunt Agatha's cottage, and they'd spent the better part of the past year remodeling the place.

"I only work half days on Friday, so I picked up Nate and we had lunch with Adrianna at the hospital."

Adrianna, Keenan knew, was Betsy's BFF, a popular nurse midwife in Jackson Hole and wife of Mayor Tripp Randall.

"How is Adrianna?" The brunette had been Betsy's friend since childhood.

"Happy." His sister's lips curved. "She and Tripp are pregnant. They just found out."

"I'll have to offer my congratulations next time I see them." Keenan struggled to grasp the reality that another of his friends was not only married, but a soon-to-be father.

Sometimes he felt as if he'd been caught in a time warp. During the period he'd spent "finding himself," his friends had somehow made the leap from impetuous boys to solid-citizens-married-with-kids. Keenan pushed the disturbing thought aside. "That still doesn't explain why you're here."

"Nate isn't a great sleeper." Betsy yawned hugely, covering her mouth with the tips of her fingers. Apparently, the little boy wasn't the only one up at night. "He fell asleep in the car on the way home from lunch. If I take him straight to the house, he wakes up. I never get him back down. So I took a drive. We ended up here."

Betsy's gaze settled on the beautiful house faced with stone and brick. "A lot of home for a single woman."

Something in his sister's tone put Keenan on alert. He was aware Betsy's husband had once dated Mitzi. Though from the rumors he'd heard it hadn't been much of a relationship, more of a brief infatuation on Ryan's part. Though Betsy was cordial to

Mitzi, there was a chasm between the two women, which he found disturbing.

He considered Mitzi a friend and wished Betsy could, too.

"It's got a great floor plan," he said, when he realized his sister expected a response.

"I was shocked when I heard Mitzi had sold her condo." Betsy took one of her son's chubby hands in hers and jiggled it. "She had a big housewarming party last year when she moved in."

Keenan simply shrugged, the up-and-down motion making Nate, who still rested on his shoulders, giggle.

"I guess I shouldn't have been surprised," Betsy said in a casual tone that he guessed was anything but casual. "That seems to be Mitzi's M.O."

Keenan cocked his head.

"She wants something," Betsy continued. "Gets it. Grows tired of it. Moves on to the next thing."

"You make these assumptions simply because Mitzi purchased a condo, decided it was a mistake then sold it to build a house?"

Betsy's widening eyes told him she'd caught the challenge in his tone.

"Not just that." His sister absently fingered a leaf on a low-hanging branch of the tree shading them. "She's like that with men, too."

"Is she?"

Betsy nodded jerkily, two bright spots of pink dotting her cheeks. "When she first came to town, she and Benedict Campbell became an item. They lasted longer than most expected. They were on and off. More off than on."

Keenan liked Ben, but it was obvious to him why he and Mitzi had split. While Ben was a nice guy, even he could see that Mitzi needed a more adventurous man. "If they didn't get along, it was good they didn't stay together."

"She and Ryan went out a few times."

Keenan's gaze met his sister's. "Before you and he got together."

"That's right," Betsy acknowledged. "Only a handful of times. Then she moved back to Ben for a while then on to Kelvin Reid."

"The NFL player." Keenan had seen the guy on television escorting an actress to some premier. *Slick* and *charming* were his impressions before he flipped the channel.

"Kelvin went out of his way to come to Jackson to see her," Betsy added. "He was even there at her condo housewarming."

"He cheated on her." Keenan's voice went flat. "She dumped him. Smart move on her part."

"Some think she's got her sights set on Winn Ferris now." Betsy's tone took on a strange urgency as a gust of wind swept up, fluttering the leaves and making Nate chortle.

He tightened his hold on the boy's chubby legs but kept his gaze firmly on his sister.

"I can't see them together," Betsy said with some reluctance. "But that's the rumor."

"Why are you telling me all this, Bets? You know I've never been one for gossip."

The flush on his sister's cheeks deepened. Still, she met his steady gaze with one of her own. "I see how you look at her when you think no one is watching."

Keenan kept his expression impassive. He'd had a lot of practice keeping his emotions under wraps. It troubled him to think his sister—and perhaps others—could read him so easily. "Tell me. How do I look at her?"

She kicked at the dirt with the toe of her shoe. "Like you want to eat her up."

"She's beautiful and charming." He kept his tone light. "What red-blooded male wouldn't?"

"But you're not in her league. That's what *she* thinks anyway."

He stilled and the air between them dipped twenty degrees.

HER KIND OF HERO | 83

Picking up on the tension in the air, the little boy began to whimper.

Betsy reached up her arms, scooped her son down from Keenan's neck. "It's okay, Nate." She set him on the ground, pulled a small ball from the oversize bag at her feet and gave it a toss. "Go get it."

The boy scrambled after the rolling ball, a wide grin on his face.

"Why do you think she's out of my league?" Keenan asked in a conversational tone.

"For goodness' sake, isn't it obvious?" Betsy flung up her hands. Frustration snapped in her voice. "Mitzi isn't like us, Keenan. She's a doctor."

He wanted to tell Betsy that if she knew Mitzi better, she'd understand the doctor wasn't that different from them. Mitzi had faced similar challenges growing up. Instead he decided to focus on the obvious. "Your husband is a lawyer."

"You know what I mean."

The blood in Keenan's veins froze. Anger and hurt warred in his gut.

"Because I'm an ex-con?" His voice was dangerously soft, flat. "Is that what you're saying?"

"I'm saying you're too good for her. You're a wonderful, caring man." Misery flooded his sister's face. "I love you so much. It would break my heart to see you hurt. After everything you've been through, you deserve only good things in your life. Only happiness."

The anger that had begun to form like a dark storm inside him dissipated as suddenly as it had begun. He gathered his sister close for a quick hug.

"Don't worry, Bets. I know the score." He kissed the top of her head before releasing her. "I've always known the score."

∼

84 | CINDY KIRK

On Friday afternoon, Mitzi drove slowly home, exhaustion seeping from every pore. She'd had to tell a working man that an amputation was necessary due to cancer spread and a twenty-year-old college sophomore that recovery from a sports injury would likely keep her from playing volleyball until next season.

On her way out the door, she was reminded she'd be handling the out-of-town clinics for the rest of the year. The first trip was scheduled next week. Mitzi loved to fly but not in small planes. Still, there was no choice. The communities they served were too far to drive.

But she refused to let something that couldn't be changed ruin what was left of the day. This evening, complete and total relaxation was the only thing on her schedule. Windsurfing with Keenan yesterday had wiped her out physically. The memory of his kisses had wiped her out emotionally.

Mitzi pulled into her driveway, already anticipating the bubble bath in her new whirlpool tub with a glass of wine for company. She paused to hit the remote button for the garage door and took the opportunity to check her online calendar to make sure she wasn't scheduled for hospital rounds tomorrow.

She inhaled sharply.

No to the hospital rounds.

Yes to a date. With Winn Ferris. Tonight. Six o'clock.

She glanced at the time and yelped. The bath and wine would be preempted by dinner, classical music and the opportunity to wear her new dress and heels.

Mitzi may have grown up knowing next to nothing of fine foods and cultural pursuits, but she'd proved a quick study. She reveled in the lifestyle her salary as an orthopedic surgeon afforded her. Now that she had more time and more money, she was determined to experience life at its fullest.

Mitzi had what her friend Kate would call an "adventurous spirit." While she loved the symphony and the opera, she'd have

HER KIND OF HERO | 85

been equally happy to toss on cowboy boots and check out a rodeo or a barn dance.

She tried to imagine Winn Ferris with a beer in one hand, hot dog in the other watching a cowboy on an eight-second ride but couldn't see it. That was okay. Not everyone was so open-minded about fun. Mitzi smiled, recalling her time with Keenan at the lake.

Windsurfing had been on her to-do list since her California days. But if Keenan hadn't encouraged her yesterday to make time for it, she still wouldn't know what a blast it could be. Kissing a handsome man while treading water had been equally fun.

She smiled as she readied herself for her date. Winn appeared to be going all out to impress her. Earlier in the week he'd told her he'd made reservations at La Maisonette, an elegant new restaurant that had opened earlier in the year. Getting the owner, a world-renowned chef, to relocate to Jackson Hole had been a real coup for the chamber of commerce.

Though Mitzi hadn't yet eaten at the restaurant, she knew what to expect: tiny bits of artistically arranged food that wasn't enough to fill up a three-pound Chihuahua. Still, she had no doubt the atmosphere would make up for the lack of quantity on the food front.

Would Winn kiss her tonight? Mitzi hoped so. Perhaps if they kissed, she'd feel a closer connection to him. Some men simply took a little more time to know.

A knock sounded on the side glass of her car. She jerked her gaze and found Keenan's hazel eyes fixed on her. Instead of rolling down the window or pulling into the garage, she pushed open the door and stepped out into the sunlight.

Mitzi took in the dusty jeans, white shirt stained with flecks of paint and frayed ball cap and resisted the urge to sigh. No man should look that good without even trying.

Then she reminded herself that Winn was hot, too.

"Hey, windsurfer dude." The teasing words came easily to her lips. "What's up?"

"It's Friday night, windsurfer chick." Amusement edged his tone. "The rodeo is in town. They always have a dance afterward. It should be fun."

An unspoken question hung in the air.

"I'm sure it will be." Mitzi felt her pulse drum. "Me, I'm headed to the symphony. That should be fun, too."

"I didn't realize Jackson Hole even had a symphony." Keenan gave a little laugh. "Tells you how far outside the loop I am. Are you going with a group of friends?"

"Actually, Winn Ferris invited me to go with him." Mitzi kept her tone light. "He has season tickets."

"Sounds like a nice evening." Keenan's smile didn't reach his eyes. "Joel asked me to work tomorrow and finish trimming out your kitchen. He said he cleared it with you."

"I'm in favor of anything that will get the house finished earlier." Only this week had Mitzi finally admitted to Kate—and Joel—she hadn't fully understood what living in a house under construction would be like. Once she'd realized how bad it was, she wanted the job completed...yesterday.

"I planned to stop by at seven." He shoved hands into his pockets, drawing her attention to the area below his belt buckle....

To that part of him that had been hard against her softness when he drew her close and they'd kissed.

"Mitzi?"

She banished the memory of how perfectly they'd fit together and smiled easily. "Seven will be fine. How was Bitty today?"

He smiled then, a warm, genuine lifting of the lips that did funny things to her insides. "She watches everything we do. If Bill is in one room and I'm in another, she divides her time. It's almost as if someone told her to keep an eye on us. Could that someone be you? Or is she Joel's spy kitty?"

Mitzi chuckled. "I'll never tell."

"Well—" Keenan rocked back on his heels "—I'd best head out. Have a nice evening."

As she watched him go, Mitzi fought a pang of regret. Though she'd never been to a rodeo or a rodeo dance, playing cowgirl and dressing in jeans and boots sounded like something she'd enjoy.

As would the symphony, Mitzi told herself and headed into the house to put on her new black party dress and heels.

CHAPTER TEN

La Maisonette wasn't actually a little room but several large ones. Elegant and romantic, the restaurant boasted linen-clad tables, baby's breath and lavender in crystal vases, and stained glass panels over a series of windows with a perfect view of the mountains.

A maître d', resplendent in a black tux, showed them to a table by one of those windows. Their server, a clean-cut college type, appeared immediately. He was attentive without being disruptive and friendly without being too familiar.

The food was exactly as Mitzi expected: a tiny piece of fish no bigger than a domino, a tablespoon of risotto, two spears of asparagus. Still, she enjoyed the meal. Winn seemed pleased when she let him order, and they chatted easily about mutual friends and upcoming events in Jackson Hole.

Mitzi was thankful Winn had a lot to say about everything. It had been a long day and she didn't feel like talking, especially not about herself. While she'd been completely honest with Keenan, for Winn she'd need to sanitize her home situation.

She'd discovered men reared in luxury often had difficulty identifying with her childhood. For the handsome man at her side, money had never been an issue. Still, it would be unfair to hold his privileged upbringing against him. Just as it had been unfair for her to hold Keenan's prison time against him, Mitzi admitted with a twinge of remorse.

Because of the symphony, they skipped dessert. They slipped into their orchestra seats at the Center for the Arts just as the curtain rose.

The concert featured American composers, and Mitzi soon lost herself in the music. She barely noticed when Winn took her hand. His palms were smooth, the nails nicely manicured and his hands free of the nicks and scratches that marred Keenan's.

She wondered if Keenan had ended up going to the rodeo, then determinedly pushed him from her mind. This was her night to build a relationship with Winn.

The business exec looked fabulous in his tailored dark suit and shiny Italian loafers. Thankfully he had splashed on different cologne tonight, a scent that actually smelled good. Unfortunately she still didn't feel the slightest zing of electricity when his thumb began to caress her palm. She told herself again that attraction often needed time to build.

After the performance, Winn asked if she wanted to stop at the Green Gateau for cappuccino and dessert.

Give him a chance, Mitzi told herself. Give him a chance to wow you.

The bistro on Scott Avenue, known for its signature green flourless torte, buzzed with activity. With warming lights taking the chill from the air, people sat outside on the patio, eating tall pieces of chocolate oblivion cake and pie with meringue a mile high.

Mitzi stepped aside while Winn opened the door. She shot him an appreciative smile as she strolled past him into the café. The man had impeccable manners.

"Looks like half the town is here," Winn joked, resting a palm lightly against the small of her back.

They slowly made their way through the milling crowd to the hostess stand, where they were informed it'd be a twenty-minute wait.

"I wonder if there is anyone here we know," Mitzi murmured. It seemed like, considering the number of people in the café.

"Good idea." Winn's gaze swept the room like a hunter in search of prey. "Bingo."

A flash of triumph filled his eyes.

Mitzi lifted a brow.

"Look who's here."

Curious now, Mitzi followed the direction of his gaze. She resisted the urge to sigh. Keenan sat with Hailey, Tripp and Adrianna at a large round table on the far side of the room.

"I'm going to see if they have room for us," Winn said almost to himself. "There's a zoning issue I'd like to discuss with our illustrious mayor, and Tripp's been a hard man to reach."

Without waiting for her response, Winn began winding his way through the tables.

So much for impeccable manners. Mitzi rolled her eyes then followed him at a sedate pace.

"We'd love to have you join us," she heard Tripp say as he pushed back his chair and smiled warmly at both her and Winn. He glanced around the table. "I believe you both know everyone."

Mitzi couldn't believe it when Winn pulled out the chair next to Keenan for her. Of course, his only other choice was to give her the seat next to Tripp. A spot he obviously had marked for himself.

"You look lovely." Adrianna's admiring gaze settled on Mitzi's retro black dress with its flared skirt and belted waist.

"Red is definitely your color," Mitzi said, returning the compliment.

Even dressed casually in jeans and a simple crimson sweater, with her sultry good looks and killer body, Adrianna was stunning.

HER KIND OF HERO | 91

"Tripp told me I couldn't wear a dress." Adrianna slipped her hand through her husband's arm, her tone teasing.

Her husband chuckled and brushed a kiss across her lips. "Who wears a dress to a rodeo?"

"The bull riding was awesome."

At the comment, Mitzi shifted her attention to Hailey. Like Adrianna, the blonde had gone casual in a Western-cut shirt that brought out the blue in her eyes. Instead of letting her hair hang loose like her sister-in-law, she'd pulled it back in a jaunty tail.

Before Mitzi could respond, Hailey shifted her focus to Keenan. "I saw Ryan ride when I was in high school. He was a-ma-zing."

Like the others at the table, Mitzi knew Ryan Harcourt had once been a champion bull rider before he quit the sport to attend law school.

"I had the biggest crush on him back then," Hailey admitted cheerfully. "All the girls did."

"I'd tell him," Keenan said, "but it'd just go to his head."

Then, Keenan's gaze settled on Mitzi. Her body began to hum as her blood warmed.

"Did you all go to the rodeo together?" Winn asked politely.

"We did." Hailey answered and shot him a bright smile.

"It was fun but I wished we'd been able to get symphony tickets." Adrianna's lips came together in a light pout. "Especially since they featured American composers this evening. Do you recall if they played Gershwin's 'An American in Paris'? It's a particular favorite of mine."

"They did. It was one of the many fine pieces they played." Winn's gaze grew thoughtful. "Copeland's 'Fanfare for the Common Man' was performed in a typically majestic fashion. And the upbeat rendition of 'Rodeo' couldn't help but lift one's spirits."

Winn glanced at Mitzi for confirmation of the recap.

She nodded, wondering if Winn had concluded the best way

92 | CINDY KIRK

to garner Tripp's favor was to impress his wife. The second the uncharitable thought surfaced, she shoved it aside.

"Even though you'd have preferred the symphony," Hailey said to her sister-in-law, "you have to admit you had fun at the rodeo."

"I did enjoy it," Adrianna admitted. "Especially seeing Cole and Meg's Charlie in the mutton-busting competition. Though I'm not sure I'd want my little boy on the back of a crazed sheep."

"I guarantee that ewe was more scared than Charlie," Tripp said with a laugh.

"Have you always been interested in music?" Winn asked Adrianna.

"I've played the flute for eons." Adrianna's expression grew wistful. "I considered making music my career, but my dad was old-school and insisted I focus on something practical."

Winn's eyes grew shuttered. "Fathers can be like that."

By the time the waiter stopped to take their order, Mitzi was engaged in a conversation with Hailey and Adrianna about an upcoming sale at a local boutique. Since she was occupied and there was very little she didn't like, Mitzi told Winn to order for her.

When Adrianna turned to greet a friend passing the table, Mitzi realized Winn had broached the zoning issue with Tripp. She felt a tap on her shoulder and turned to Keenan.

She let her gaze linger for just a second and felt a little shiver. His military-green Henley stretched wide over muscled shoulders. He'd pushed the sleeves up, showing strong arms with a light dusting of hair. Even though he was dressed casually and his hair was in tousled disarray, there wasn't a more handsome man at the table.

"Fried banana with coconut ice cream?" Keenan's lips twitched.

At first she didn't understand. Then it hit her. "Is that what Winn ordered for me?"

HER KIND OF HERO | 93

"I chose the chocolate oblivion. If you're nice to me, I might give you a bite." A devilish gleam sparkled in Keenan's hazel eyes. "Unless you think you'll be too full after eating all that *coconut* ice cream."

"Ha, ha." Mitzi narrowed her gaze. The chocolate oblivion was a personal favorite. And for her, one taste would never be enough. "Let's...negotiate. I give you all of the coconut ice cream."

"So generous," he said, stifling a smile.

"I'll even toss in the fried banana."

"Gee, thanks."

This time, Mitzi was the one who struggled not to smile.

"And you get what in exchange?" Keenan prompted when she didn't immediately make her demand.

Mitzi cast a sideways glance. Winn was still engaged in an animated conversation with Tripp. Her date was so busy trying to impress Tripp, she doubted he'd even notice she was eating a different dessert than he'd ordered.

Coconut ice cream?

Fried banana?

What had the man been thinking? Still, if Keenan agreed to her terms, a happy ending was still in reach.

"Just half your cake," she said quickly. "Not much considering all I'm giving you."

"No deal," Keenan said. "One bite. And that's if you're nice to me."

She snorted. "I'm always nice to you."

Unexpectedly he smiled. "Yes," he said. "You are."

Though she could have pressed the cake issue, she decided to regroup then circle back. "You never mentioned you were going to the rodeo with the Randalls."

"I went with Betsy and Ryan. We ran into Hailey, Tripp and Adrianna when we got there and decided to sit together." Keenan lifted a shoulder in a slight shrug. "Betsy and Ry headed straight home afterward because they had a sitter with a curfew. The rest of us came here for dessert."

"I'm glad you did," she said in an offhand tone, then stared down when the waitress put the huge chunk of chocolate cake in front of him.

Keenan shot a glance at Winn, who was still engaged in an earnest discussion with Tripp, complete with hand gestures and intense voices.

"Since you're sacrificing your Saturday for my house, come early. I'll make you breakfast." Mitzi wasn't sure who was most surprised by the impulsive offer, her or Keenan. "Do you like huevos rancheros?"

"Love 'em." He picked up his fork, looked at her. "I'll need coffee with those eggs. Strong and black."

"You're very particular."

Keenan's smile came slow. "Let's just say I'm a man who knows what he wants."

Mitzi hummed the next morning as she chopped chilies, made sauce and cooked tortillas. Once that was done, she ground beans and set the coffee to brew before grabbing eggs from the refrigerator. She paused before cracking them, her thoughts drifting.

After leaving the café, Winn had driven her home. She'd invited him in and given him the grand tour. Once that was done, they'd done a little kissing.

The man knew how to kiss, she'd give him that. The problem was with her. Though she tried to muster some enthusiasm, she'd felt nothing. Nada. Not one spark.

Her reaction made Mitzi wonder if the problem lay with Winn or her. Was her lack of desire a result of zero chemistry between them? Or did the complete absence of sexual energy go deeper?

HER KIND OF HERO | 95

From what she recalled, that hadn't been an issue any of the times she and Keenan had kissed. Unless her memory was playing tricks on her.

She might need to see about a repeat performance. Purely for scientific research purposes, of course. *Kisses for eggs?*

Mitzi smiled and picked up the wooden spoon. She stirred the simmering sauce.

"Something smells mighty good in here."

Mitzi jumped. The spoon flew from her hand to clatter on the floor. She whirled. "Keenan. You startled me."

Dressed in faded jeans and a white T-shirt with scarred leather work boots on his feet, Keenan looked rough, rugged and mouthwateringly good.

"I knocked a couple of times but you didn't hear me." Keenan crossed the room and silenced the jarring beat of a Metallica guitar riff blaring from the radio.

"What can I say? I like heavy metal and I like it loud." She grinned.

He glanced around the kitchen just in time to see Bitty tear into the room as if her tail was on fire. She slid across the quarry tile floor with front paws extended.

Mitzi chuckled. "Welcome to my world. She does this all the time."

Keenan scooped up the kitten, held out the tiny bundle of gray fur and studied her with a critical eye. "Itty Bitty is getting fat."

"No surprise. She eats like a pig." Mitzi picked up the spoon from the floor and set it in the sink. After wiping up the mess, she grabbed another from a drawer. "If any mice snuck into the house during construction, they're safe. This little piggy, er, kitty, isn't hungry enough to go after them."

Keenan drew the animal to him, stroking it until it began to purr. "Will Winn be joining us?"

96 | CINDY KIRK

Mitzi frowned. "I didn't invite him to come by. Did you have something you needed to discuss with him?"

"Not really," Keenan said cheerfully.

It wasn't until Mitzi cracked the last egg into the skillet that the implication struck her. "You wanted to know if he spent the night."

"Don't get your nose out of joint." Keenan set Bitty on the floor. "I just needed to know if I had to be all cultured and on my best behavior this morning. For instance, if he was here, I couldn't do this—"

Swiping the spoon from her hand, he dipped it into the sauce of tomatoes and green chilies for a taste. "That's good stuff."

Swatting his arm, she jerked the spoon from his hand. "Stop that."

Looking not at all repentant, Keenan sidled over to the coffeemaker. He poured two cups of the steaming brew, keeping one for himself and handing the other to Mitzi.

While she fried the eggs, he leaned against the counter, looking way sexier than any man had a right so early in the morning. She'd gone for casual this morning: a pair of black knit pants and a cashmere top in emerald-green. Her hair tumbled loose around her shoulders, but she'd pulled the strands back from her face with a thin tortoise-shell band.

After taking a long sip of the strong Columbian blend, Mitzi set out the plates of food and gestured for him to sit.

He pulled out a chair. "Ladies first."

For several minutes they ate in comfortable silence. Then she mentioned something about work and he told her about his conversation with Ben. Mitzi realized she'd never asked about his progress toward getting back in the air. "Did you get your pilot's license?"

The smile that spread across his face gave her the answer before he even spoke. "I did. Yes, I did."

"Will you be quitting your job with Joel?"

"I wish I could." He put down his fork. "It's not that I don't enjoy working for Joel. I do. He's a great guy. And the job gives me a steady income. But flying is my passion. And I'm determined to find a way to do it full-time."

Mitzi understood. Medicine had always been her passion. She'd set a goal of becoming an orthopedic surgeon and that had been that.

Now, she was ready to move on to the next item on her list. She had her career. A new home. Now she wanted a husband.

Her analysis indicated Winn Ferris would be the perfect choice. If only she was attracted to him.

She gazed across the table at Keenan. His hair was longer, brushing his collar. And the fingers holding a fork, instead of being perfectly manicured, were clean but battle-scarred and rough.

What would it feel like to have that hand glide across her skin and cup her breast? Her breath hitched. She forced herself to take a sip of coffee, tried to concentrate on the hearty breakfast. But she couldn't banish the image, couldn't stop the ache that formed low in her belly.

She told herself this was all because Winn's kisses last night had left her cold and frustrated. She'd blown her experience with Keenan out of proportion. Now she couldn't get him out of her mind.

There was only one way to deal with the matter. She was going to have to kiss Keenan again.

CHAPTER ELEVEN

Several times during breakfast, Keenan caught Mitzi staring. He wondered if he'd missed a spot when he shaved that morning or if he hadn't quite gotten all the mahogany stain off his neck during his shower.

But he got the feeling the doctor wasn't sitting back, judging him, she was...desiring him.

It had been a long time since Keenan had a pretty girl look at him that way, but a guy didn't forget.

Still, Mitzi had been with Winn Ferris less than twenty-four hours earlier. Attending the symphony, for chrissakes. She'd looked incredibly hot in that jet-black dress and spiky heels. And elegant and unattainable with her hair all twisted up. She'd been acting strange, too.

When she'd let Winn order for her, like some docile society drone, he'd wondered if an alien had taken over her body. Especially when the guy had ordered a dessert containing coconut, which even he knew she despised.

But when Winn had gotten drawn into that discussion with Tripp, he'd discovered the Mitzi who fascinated him, who bedazzled him, was still there, well hidden under a stylish exterior.

HER KIND OF HERO | 99

"For now, keeping your current job makes sense," she agreed. "But I bet you have a plan to get a flying gig."

"Bill's brother, Steve, runs a charter service." Keenan lifted his attention from Mitzi's luscious red lips to her eyes. "He's hired me to help out as needed. As long as I give him notice, Joel says I can take off whenever I get the opportunity to fly."

"That's nice of him." Mitzi placed her fork on the table and stared at him.

Her gaze appeared focused on his jaw. No, not on his jaw. On his mouth.

A quick burst of heat singed his insides. She was a client, he reminded himself. He was here to finish trimming out the kitchen. "Thanks for the breakfast."

"Thanks for the cake last night."

"Watching you devour most of that piece was my pleasure." He'd found the sight of those full red lips closing over a forkful of rich dark chocolate incredibly arousing.

Reluctantly, Keenan pushed back his chair. As he took his plate to the sink, he felt her gaze follow him.

When he turned, she was right there. She smelled as good as she looked. Like the wildflowers that had grown in his backyard when he was a child.

"What's your hurry?" She spoke in a low, sultry voice that reminded him of tangled sheets and naked bodies.

Keenan forced a weak grin, tapped the scarred watch on his wrist. "On the clock."

"I have something to ask you." Her vivid blue eyes were serious.

"Ask away."

"Will you kiss me?"

Keenan stared, certain he'd heard incorrectly. "Pardon?"

"I asked you to kiss me." Irritation skittered across her face. "What's so hard to understand?"

"You were with Winn last night. Didn't he satisfy you?"

At her quick intake of breath, Keenan cursed himself for a fool. It wasn't his business what she did or didn't do with Winn Ferris.

She startled him when she laughed. "You're very perceptive."

What the heck did that mean? Keenan didn't have time to do more than wonder because her arms were suddenly around his neck and her mouth on his.

Even if he'd wanted, he couldn't have resisted the pull. They were two magnets drawn together with impossible force.

Her lips were warm and sweet, and he let his mouth linger. The kiss started out gentle, a simple kiss between friends. It quickly morphed into more. A tangible connection of feelings he could no longer deny.

Keenan settled his hands on her hips, molding her soft body against his hard one. They fit together perfectly.

His tongue swept across her lips, and when she opened her mouth to him, he deepened the kiss. It was as if a tank of fuel exploded inside him. Suddenly close wasn't close enough. He wanted to crawl inside her skin, bury himself in her, kiss her for the rest of eternity.

Her back was to the counter and she began to squirm as they continued to kiss, chest rising and falling. His hand slid up her side to cup her breast, his thumb teasing her nipple to a point through the thin fabric of her shirt.

He cursed the fabric separating them. He wanted to feel her warm flesh beneath the palm of his hand, taste the sweetness against his tongue. Pushing her shirt up, he shoved the tiny scrap of fabric covering her breasts aside, intent on replacing his fingers with his mouth.

Before that could happen she grabbed his hair, pulled his head up.

"Stop," she said with eyes wide, cheeks flushed. "You have to stop."

HER KIND OF HERO | 101

He longed to ignore the request, but he'd never forced a woman and he wasn't about to start now.

With Herculean effort, he stepped back, bent over and rested his hands on his thighs, ignoring the aching in his groin as he fought for control.

"What the hell just happened?" he muttered with a laugh that held little humor.

"Flash point." She raked a trembling hand through her hair. "I guess it wasn't me after all."

Something in her tone cut through the fog.

"What are you talking about?"

"When I kissed Winn last night I felt nothing." She was chattering, he realized, almost as if she was as off-balanced as he. "But you. Well, I thought that had been a fluke. That it hadn't been good, but it had. You've got great moves."

The last of the fog disappeared, swept away by a gust of irritation. "Is that what this was?" He gestured between them. "An experiment?"

She didn't appear to notice the edge to his voice. "I had to know."

"So you go out in public with your fancy business executive then invite me to breakfast when you want to go slumming?"

"What?" Her brows pulled together as if he was speaking a language she didn't understand. "No. What are you saying? Of course not. Like I said, I—"

"I heard very clearly what you said." His tone was ice and he didn't bother to civilize it. Keenan fixed his gaze on hers and held.

"I grew up feeling second best, like I wasn't good enough." He gave a harsh laugh. "It took me a lot of years and a whole bunch of growing up to realize that I play second string to no one. If you want someone to heat up your sheets in secret, *Doctor* Sanchez, look somewhere else."

Without looking back, he called over his shoulder. "I'm going to work. Do me a favor and stay out of my way."

On Sunday afternoon, Mitzi spilled just the basics of her story to Kate while they shopped. By her friend's lack of response, she assumed she'd shocked her BFF silent.

But when Kate began to giggle, Mitzi raised an indignant brow. "What's so funny?"

"The image of you feeding Keenan, then jumping him..." Kate dissolved into laughter.

"I don't see what's so funny," Mitzi said, even as her own lips curved.

"Seduction over huevos rancheros," Kate intoned, her eyes sparkling. "Wouldn't that make a fabulous title? I'd love to read that one for book club. Especially the love scene."

"Shut up, Kate," Mitzi said mildly.

"It's such a guy thing," her friend drawled. "Ply a woman with good food then jump her bones."

"I didn't jump Keenan." Mitzi's voice had started to rise. When the clerk glanced her way, she lowered it and pretended to be studying the rack of clothes. "I kissed him. And I told you the reason. You weren't listening."

"I was listening all right." Kate smothered a smile. "But c'mon, Mitzi. You can't actually expect me to believe the only reason you jumped, er, kissed, Keenan was to test your sexual urges."

This time it was Kate who spoke too loud. The last two words had not only the clerk but a bright-eyed customer glancing in their direction.

Mitzi grabbed her friend's arm, smiled grimly as she hauled Kate from the store and into the sunshine. "If we're going to talk sexual urges, we're going to do it outside where we can't be overheard."

HER KIND OF HERO | 103

Amusement tugged at the corners of Kate's lips. "I do believe you're embarrassed, Dr. Sanchez."

With more than a little exasperation, Mitzi pushed back her hair as the two women strode down the sidewalk, heels clicking smartly.

Mitzi glanced around to make sure no one was close enough to overhear. "You can't tell anyone what I'm about to tell you, not even Joel."

Just as Mitzi anticipated, Kate hesitated. She and her husband didn't keep secrets. Not since a secret Kate had withheld had almost derailed their relationship.

"I wouldn't ask if it wasn't important, Kate," Mitzi said, her voice earnest. "But Keenan works for Joel and this is...personal."

Mitzi could see her friend looking back almost a dozen years, to when Kate had given birth over summer break and kept it a secret from her medical school classmates. Only Mitzi had known. She'd never breathed a word.

"Tell me." Kate focused her hazel eyes on Mitzi. "I won't say a word to anyone."

Having the reassurance she sought, she took Kate's arm and directed her into a small park enclosed in a gleaming black wrought iron fence tipped with gold.

"I come here sometimes during the week to eat my lunch," Mitzi said in response to Kate's raised eyebrow. "I try to time it when there aren't a lot of kids here."

"I bet that's difficult," Kate said with a wry smile. "Considering it's a *park*."

A park where, even now, toddlers and preschool-age children climbed brightly colored slides and swung high into the air emitting shrieks of laughter.

Mitzi kept walking until they reached a bench as far as possible from the children's play area. Here, manicured bushes in the shape of animals stood tall on both sides of them, muting the noise.

104 | CINDY KIRK

Once Kate had taken a seat beside her, Mitzi swiveled to face her. "You know what it was like for me growing up."

"I've always admired your determination to rise above such humble beginnings."

"I got out, stayed out and succeeded in life because I've stuck to my plan." Mitzi blew out a breath. "That's why focusing on Winn made such sense."

Kate smiled encouragingly.

"Keenan isn't on my list. He isn't settled. He's still in that having-fun stage. Did I tell you he took me windsurfing at Lake Jackson?" Mitzi confessed with all the seriousness of saying he'd robbed a bank.

"Life isn't all serious, Mitzi. Joel and I have lots of fun—" Kate stopped speaking when her friend abruptly stood and began to pace.

"I've already told you some of what happened that morning, but not all." Mitzi flung out her hands, her emotions as muddied as her thoughts. Beneath the anger that flashed in Keenan's eyes, she'd seen pain. Pain *she'd* caused. Her heart twisted. "He thinks I don't want to be seen with him, Kate."

Confusion furrowed Kate's brow. "Why would he think that?"

For Kate to understand, Mitzi had to hold nothing back. The confession came out in a torrent of words. Her voice faltered when she spoke of the look she'd seen in Keenan's eyes when he'd accused her of being ashamed of him.

"As you can see, my actions were calculating and—" Mitzi swallowed hard past the sudden lump in her throat "—heartless."

Kate placed a hand on Mitzi's arm, her eyes filled with sympathy. "A bit calculating, I'll grant you. But not heartless."

"I could never be ashamed of Keenan," Mitzi said, her voice cracking. "He's a great guy. He's handsome, smart and incredibly kind. Keenan risked his own life to save Itty Bitty."

Mitzi took a moment to fill Kate in on Keenan's heart-stopping rescue of the gray kitten.

HER KIND OF HERO | 105

"That's amazing. Bitty is a very lucky cat."

"I love her," Mitzi said simply.

"I wondered where you and Keenan went when you left the house." Kate's lips tipped in a smile. "I'd never have guessed *there.*"

"Keenan has to watch his pennies until he gets back on his feet," Mitzi said. "Eating samples on Tuesday night is one way to stretch a paycheck."

"That was nice of you," Kate murmured, eying her. "And so helpful."

"He'd do the same for me. He's that way."

"A good guy, you said."

"*Great* guy," Mitzi clarified. "None better."

Kate nodded, but remained silent. It was as if she knew there was more Mitzi still hadn't shared.

"When I realized I'd hurt him..." Mitzi blew out a breath, spread her hands and let them drop. She was stunned to feel tears sting her eyes. She blinked them back before Kate could notice.

All light had left Kate's face. She stroked Mitzi's arm, her eyes dark and filled with concern. In the distance a baby cried and a toddler's high-pitched giggle drifted on the breeze.

"Before now I never gave any of the men I dated a second thought." Mitzi gave a strangled laugh. "I don't know what's gotten into me. The funny thing is, I'm not even dating Keenan, not really."

"He's more than just a date," Kate ventured. "He's a friend."

"He was..." Mitzi's voice trailed off as a wave of sadness washed over her.

"You know what you need to do." Though Kate spoke softly, Mitzi heard clearly.

"Apologize." Mitzi sighed. "Yes, I know."

"You'll both feel better when you do."

There was only one problem. She met Kate's gaze. "I've never apologized to a man before."

Surprise skittered across Kate's face. "Never?"

"Never."

Kate looped an arm around Mitzi's shoulders, gave a squeeze. "There's a first time for everything."

With her emotions still in turmoil, bright and early Monday morning, Mitzi headed to the private airstrip, prepared for another long day. She'd filled in once or twice at the satellite orthopedic clinics the group did in small towns across Wyoming and knew what to expect. A quick plane ride. A day of seeing patients. Then back to Jackson Hole before dark.

She'd left home before any of the workmen had arrived. When she turned out of her housing area and onto the highway, she was embarrassed to admit, she'd breathed a sigh of relief. Though Mitzi knew it was cowardly, she didn't feel up to seeing Keenan this morning.

She would set things right between them. She would apologize. But not today. Her earlier awkward attempt told her it was best she take time to formulate and refine exactly what she wanted to say. If she didn't, she might make things worse. Though it was hard to imagine how it could be any worse.

Mitzi hadn't heard from Keenan since he'd left her house Saturday. Bitty missed him. And so did she.

After parking her car in the gravel lot, Mitzi made a beeline for Hangar 4. It wasn't that she was eager to fly. She simply wanted the day over so she could be alone with her thoughts. Perhaps she'd make a list of things to include in her apology. She smiled, feeling better now that she had a plan.

The five-seater parked outside the hangar looked incredibly small, which made her doubly grateful for the clear skies overhead.

Mitzi loved to fly.

Just not in bad weather.

Especially not in small planes.

The pilot cut a fine sight. At least, she assumed the man bent over performing the last-minute checks to the aircraft was who'd be taking her to Delano today. His well-worn jeans encased long legs and the chambray shirt stretched across broad shoulders.

"Good morning." She spoke in a voice loud enough to be heard over the planes landing and taking off nearby.

The man straightened and turned. For a split second Mitzi forgot how to breathe.

"Hi, Mitzi." Keenan's smile didn't quite reach his eyes. "I'll be your pilot today."

Mitzi stared. Was this a joke? Then she remembered him telling her he'd gotten his license.

"Dr. Sanchez." Steve Kowalksi hurried up, a big smile on his face. "I see you've met Keenan."

"I have." Mitzi cleared her throat. "I thought Ben said Tom Rex would be taking me to Delano today."

"Tommy called in sick this morning." Steve offered a look of apology. "His kids had the flu last week. Now he's got it."

"Oh," was all Mitzi said.

Picking up on the tension, Steve glanced between Mitzi and Keenan. "Mr. McGregor is a competent pilot, Dr. Sanchez. But I can understand if you don't want to fly with someone new."

Though Keenan stood rigid and his expression gave nothing away, a tiny muscle twitched in his jaw. Mitzi knew what this chance meant to him.

But they would be alone in the plane, with too much time to talk about an incident she wasn't sure she was ready to discuss.

Would it really be so wrong to reschedule?

CHAPTER TWELVE

Though a hard knot had formed in the pit of his stomach, Keenan forced a calm expression. When Steve had called this morning and asked if he could help out, Keenan hadn't hesitated. This was the chance he'd been waiting for, an opportunity to show he could do the job, a chance to get back in the air and be paid for doing something he loved.

The fact that the day had been bright and sunny appeared a good omen. Then he'd gotten the paperwork and saw Spring Gulch Orthopedics on the list. His heart had sunk but he'd reassured himself that Mitzi wasn't the only orthopedic surgeon in the practice.

Though Keenan recalled Ben mentioning that Mitzi would be doing more of these rural clinics, what were the odds she'd be on this flight?

Now, here she stood, hair pulled back in some kind of twist, looking coolly professional in dark pants and a crisp white shirt, staring at him with an inscrutable expression and holding his fate in her hands. While that might seem a bit melodramatic, Steve Kowalski was a businessman. If he got the slightest whiff that patrons of his charter service might not accept Keenan as their pilot, he'd be out.

But he'd be damned if he'd grovel or beg. Keenan met that inscrutable gaze with a challenging one of his own.

"Of course there's no problem." Mitzi flashed a bright smile. "I was simply surprised. There's no one I'd trust more with my life than Mr. McGregor."

A look of relief skittered across Steve's face. When he spoke, his booming voice was hearty. "That's what we like to hear."

Steve slapped Keenan on the back. "Have a good flight."

He walked off, leaving Keenan alone with Mitzi.

Keenan automatically held out a hand. "Let me stow your bag."

Mitzi pulled the bag close to her chest as if it were a shield. "I can handle it."

Yes, she could handle the bag and whatever got tossed her way. She was tough. It was only one of her many characteristics he admired.

The question was could *he* handle it? Keenan had done a good job of putting the incident in the kitchen out of his head. Up to this point, he thought he'd been equally efficient in banishing her from his heart.

But now, having her gaze at him with those cool blue eyes, feeling the familiar heat that surged whenever she was near, made him realize he'd been fooling himself. He hadn't forgotten anything. It was all there, bubbling like a pot of stew, ready to spill over.

But Keenan refused to let his personal life encroach on his workday.

Today was business. All business.

Mitzi obviously understood that, too, because she'd told Steve flying with him wasn't an issue. He would never admit that at her words, the air had left his lungs and his knees had wobbled at her declaration. His immediate future rode on Steve believing he could keep the clients happy.

That's why he would bury any irritation and make sure this was a good trip for her. He finished checking out the aircraft then helped Mitzi inside the small plane. After making sure she was settled in and ready, they headed down the runway.

The simple act of rising into the air was such a thrill that Keenan forgot everything else and simply reveled in the moment. This was what he was born to do. Flying was the ultimate freedom. When he was high above the earth, it was as if the world stretched out before him. His for the taking.

"Will it take long to reach Delano?" Mitzi spoke loudly over the engine noise.

"We should be there in forty-five." More relaxed now, and fully in control of his emotions, Keenan ventured a sideways glance. "Do you have many patients to see?"

"From the list they gave me of appointments, it looks like a full schedule." She settled back against the leather seat and her hands unclenched. "Makes the trip worth the time."

The fact that there wasn't the slightest hint of snippiness in her tone told him she wouldn't make the trip miserable simply because they'd had a falling out.

"Who are these patients you'll be seeing?"

"They've all been evaluated by their family doc, and some kind of orthopedic surgery is being considered. I'll examine them, review their records then decide if I believe surgery is indicated." She met his gaze. "A lot of patients think that because I'm a surgeon, I'll push to cut. That's not the case."

"How did you decide on your specialty?" he asked politely. She was the client, and friendly conversation was part of the service.

"Bones and joints always interested me." She shrugged. "Not a very girly thing, but I love it."

HER KIND OF HERO | 111

"You followed your dream," he said. "You should be proud of yourself."

"Keenan."

His stomach clenched at the tremor in her voice. He tightened his fingers on the yoke. "Yes?"

"I'm sorry about what happened the other day."

Shock held him silent for a second. When he started to speak, she talked over him.

"I know how it appeared." Her words came out in a rush. "I know what I said, what you thought, but it's not true."

Keenan didn't want to discuss her foolishness in focusing on a man who didn't have an adventurous bone in his body. Not only that, she'd practically come out and said the guy didn't turn her on. And if she was thinking of heating up the sheets with him, Keenan had made it clear he wasn't interested in playing secret lover. What more was there to say? "Let it drop."

"I won't." She rested a hand on his bare forearm, scorching him with her touch. "I can't."

"Okay," he said equitably, his voice calm even as his heart jackhammered against his ribs. "Say what you want to say. *Then* we'll drop it."

"I'm thirty-four years old, Keenan. I've achieved all of the goals I've set so far. One by one I've crossed them off."

"Next up is finding a husband," he said, unable to keep the censure from his tone.

She lifted her chin. "That's right."

"And you really believe Winn Ferris can make you happy?"

"I don't," Mitzi said. "That's why Winn is off the list."

Keenan pulled his brows together, not sure he'd heard correctly. "List?"

"Husband list," she clarified. "I believe in being organized and methodical in my approach to a goal."

"A list," he repeated and shook his head.

"It makes sense," she insisted. "Take Winn for example. The

chemistry was definitely not there. I tried to give him the benefit of the doubt because he was perfect in so many other ways. I thought it might be me. But—"

"There's chemistry between us," Keenan interrupted before she could bring up what had happened in the kitchen. "Where do I rank on your list?"

The question popped out before he could stop it.

"You're not on it."

Keenan ignored the sharp pain in his gut and kept his tone conversational. "Why not?"

"You want to have your own plane, your own charter service eventually."

"True. But what does that have to do with your list?"

"You've got the drive and ambition to make that happen. But right now you're where I was several years ago, working long hours for not a lot of money but with eyes focused firmly on the brass ring. You're not ready to settle down." A shadow stole across her face but was gone so quickly he wondered if he'd only imagined it. "I'm looking for a guy who has grabbed hold of his dreams and is ready for a wife and a family. Right now. Not someday."

"It makes sense," Keenan said grudgingly.

"Though I meant no harm, I realize now that I was wrong to use you the way I did. I hope you can forgive me." She tilted her head back, her eyes meeting his. "I hope we can continue to be friends. Your friendship means a lot to me."

She looked so worried, it took everything he had not to pull her into his arms and comfort. Instead he chuckled. "Does anyone ever stay mad at you?"

"Oh, definitely," she admitted with a rueful smile. "But I hope not you."

"I appreciate you telling Steve you trusted me to fly you to Delano."

"I meant what I said." A wistful quality filled her voice. "Given the choice, there's no one I'd rather be with than you."

Once she reached the small health center in the center of town, Mitzi was ushered to the back. She quickly discovered the schedule of patients she'd been given had been a "preliminary" one.

"I planned to fly back at three," Mitzi told the nurse, her brows pulling together at the long list of names.

"We'll do our best to get you out of here by then, doctor." The older woman, who wore the starched white uniform reminiscent of a bygone era and a cap, as well, gestured to a door. "The first patient is in exam room two."

Before entering the room, Mitzi texted Keenan and informed him they might not be ready to leave as early as they'd hoped.

By three o'clock, the waiting room still teemed with patients waiting to be seen, some of whom Mitzi knew had driven several hours for their appointment. When she contacted Keenan to inform him they'd have to delay their flight back, he warned a storm was moving in.

She finished seeing the last patient at five. Outside, the blue skies had turned an ominous gray. When she reached the airstrip, she got the bad news. There were more storms between Delano and Jackson Hole. Though it hadn't yet started to rain in Delano, because of the wind gusts and lightning, flying wasn't recommended.

"We'll have to spend the night." Keenan glanced around the inside of the small hangar. "I can bunk here. We'll have to find a place for you."

Mitzi stared at the concrete floor, wondering just where he planned to sleep. After making several calls, Mitzi discovered the only motel in town was full but found a B and B with one room left.

Keenan walked Mitzi to the Country Dreams B and B, a quaint two-story with lots of gingerbread molding. The yard, surrounded by a white picket fence, held more wildflowers than grass. A path of stepping-stones led to the steps of the wrap-around porch.

The proprietor, a stout woman in her early fifties, opened the door before they could knock and greeted them warmly. She pressed a key in Mitzi's hand, apologized for the need to hurry off and advised tonight she was making dinner for the guests. It would be on the table in thirty minutes.

Keenan turned to leave but Mitzi took his hand and pulled him up the stairs with her. When they reached the room, she motioned him inside.

He smiled. "Let me guess. You need me to make sure there are no monsters hiding under the bed?"

She shoved him none too gently into the room, then shut the door and fixed on a stern look. "Look, we both know it's going to be miserable for you in that hangar."

"Have you ever slept in a cell?"

She ignored the comment and gestured to the lovely though decidedly feminine room. To the brass bed topped with a wedding-ring quilt. To the lace doilies and bud vases with flowers scattered throughout the room. "This would be much more comfortable."

He quirked a brow. "Why, Dr. Sanchez, are you inviting me to sleep with you?"

"*Sleep* being the operative word," Mitzi said drily. "Be sensible, Keenan. Stay. Have a nice dinner. Enjoy a good night's sleep. We'll head out in the morning, relaxed and refreshed."

A crack of thunder punctuated her words. Almost immediately, waves of rain began beating against the windowpanes.

She shifted her gaze back to Keenan and cocked her head.

HER KIND OF HERO | 115

He smiled, a lazy lifting of the lips that did crazy things to her insides. "I may be many things, but I'm not a fool."

Capturing her hand, he brought it to his lips and brushed a kiss across her knuckles. "I'd be delighted to spend the night with you."

≈

Keenan followed Mitzi down the stairs to the dining room and wondered just when he'd lost his mind. Hadn't he decided it would be best to keep his relationship with Mitzi strictly professional?

Granted, there was that blasted electricity crackling in the air whenever she got within ten feet of him, but she'd been right. He had plans for his life. Before he could even consider becoming involved in a serious relationship, he had goals to pursue. And obtain.

But to spend the night with a beautiful woman and not touch...a man would have to be a saint. No one, absolutely no one, had ever accused Keenan McGregor of being a saint.

Still, the room was warm and dry and he'd get two good meals out of the deal. Surely he could keep his hands to himself for one night.

"Keenan is a friend," Mitzi was telling Mrs. Thompsett, the proprietor, "and an excellent pilot. He flew me here."

"Isn't that nice?" Mrs. Thompsett, as round as she was tall, smiled warmly at him before refocusing on Mitzi.

Though Mitzi still wore the black pants and white shirt she'd had on this morning, seeing her without her lab coat made her look less like a doctor and more like a desirable woman.

"My neighbor Mrs. Clara Wilks had been looking forward to her appointment for weeks." Mrs. Thompsett's eyes sparkled with interest. "Did you recommend surgery?"

"Everything concerning any patient I see is confidential."

116 | CINDY KIRK

Mitzi made a zipping motion across her mouth. "My lips are sealed."

Still, Keenan noted she said it with such good nature that Mrs. Thompsett didn't take offense. Instead the older woman's eyes twinkled. "I'll call her after dinner and get the scoop."

She gestured to a large oval table topped with a lace tablecloth where several people already sat. "Have a seat and get acquainted."

After introducing themselves, Keenan pulled out Mitzi's chair then sat beside her. It didn't take long to learn that one of the couples was in town visiting friends while the other were tourists passing through.

Mitzi chatted easily. Keenan had heard the doctor called a chameleon, a woman who changed to fit her circumstances. He'd observed that firsthand when he'd seen her with Winn after the symphony.

Keenan had to wonder who Mitzi was when she was with him and who she'd be tonight. And which one was the real Mitzi Sanchez.

Dinner ended up being a pleasant affair. The other couples were interesting and the food top-notch. From fresh garden salad accompanied by flaky dinner rolls to beef Wellington, everything was melt-in-your-mouth good.

Though it probably wasn't apparent to anyone at the table but her, Mitzi felt Keenan's eyes on her. When she waited to eat until the hostess had picked up her fork, he also waited.

She understood. For years she'd read and studied proper etiquette. If she was going to rise above her initial station in life, she had to be prepared. That preparation included knowing the correct way to set a table, what utensils to use and how to choose the proper wine.

The last wasn't an issue for Keenan. Unlike Mitzi and the others at the table, her pilot chose iced tea over wine. She sipped her glass of red and turned to him.

HER KIND OF HERO | 117

"I'm warning you. After all this delicious food, I may be over the weight limit tomorrow." She gazed at Keenan over the rim of her cut-crystal wineglass. "Be thinking of what we can leave behind."

"I'd say we could take a walk and work some of it off, but—" his gaze shifted to the large bay window currently being pelted by sprays of rain "—I think we're stuck inside for the evening."

Jolene—of Sig and Jolene—must have been listening because she tapped Mitzi on the arm. "We were talking before you two sat down." Jolene glanced over at the other couple, who'd introduced themselves as Perry and Liz. "We thought it'd be fun to play a few hands of cards after dinner. Interested in joining us?"

Mitzi wasn't good at cards. She didn't know very many games, and those she had played she barely remembered. Yet, she swallowed the excuse that had begun to form on her lips. What was her alternative? Go up to the bedroom with Keenan? And do what?

Though she'd acted as if sleeping in the same room with him was no big deal, even as she'd issued the invitation, Mitzi had known she was playing with fire. There was no denying the sexually charged chemistry between them. Common sense told her the less time they spent in the room alone, the better.

Sleep with him. No strings.

The thought tempted, teased and was deliberately and harshly discarded.

Not an option, she told herself.

"It should be loads of fun," Liz added, her smile warm and friendly.

"What card game are you playing?" Mitzi asked.

"Pitch," Jolene said promptly. "Since there're six of us, we could play 'Call for your partner.'"

They might as well have been speaking a foreign language.

"I only know how to play poker," Keenan admitted.

Mitzi wrinkled her nose. "I'm afraid—"

118 | CINDY KIRK

"Don't you two worry none." Jolene waved away their concern. "It's super easy to learn. My goodness, anyone who can make it through medical school or fly a plane can learn to play a simple card game."

It was close to eleven by the time Mitzi and Keenan stood, despite the protests of the other couples, to head upstairs.

Though the rain continued to beat a relentless rhythm against the windows and the sides of the house, inside it remained dry and cozy.

"Simple game, my ass," Keenan muttered once they left the dining room.

Mitzi offered him a sympathetic look. "Forget Jolene's whining. Bidding seven on an ace then calling for the three wasn't reckless."

Keenan unexpectedly smiled, looking surprisingly pleased with himself. "If she could have gotten to me with that number two scoring pencil, I think she'd have stabbed me."

"My impression," Mitzi told him as she stepped aside and he unlocked the bedroom door with the old-fashioned key, "is that Jolene likes to complain. Still, seeing her give you the stink-eye was amusing."

Keenan grimaced and dropped into a nearby chair. "Playing was fun for a while. Toward the last I was ready to be done with it. There seemed to be no end in sight."

"You deliberately went set." The realization washed over her. "And took Jolene down with you."

"The fact she had the three was icing on the cake." He kicked off his boots, propped his feet up on a hassock topped with needlepoint. His lips spread in a wide grin. "No need to thank me."

Impulsively, Mitzi crossed the room and brushed a kiss across his lips. "Thank you, anyway."

His hazel eyes focused on her as she sauntered away. "Hey, where are you going?"

"Shower." She scooped up a white nightie from the bed. "Knowing we didn't have anything to sleep in, Mrs. Thompsett gave you pajamas and me a nightgown."

"I don't wear pajamas," he called out.

"You do tonight," Mitzi said and pulled the bathroom door shut.

CHAPTER THIRTEEN

The warm water from the shower relaxed Mitzi and the rose-scented lotion soothed her skin. She slipped into the white night-gown, relieved to discover it wasn't quite as sheer as she first feared.

Of course, the safest thing would probably be to sleep in her clothes. *Safe.* She snorted. How ridiculous to have reached the ripe old age of thirty-four and be apprehensive about spending the night with a man.

If they had sex, it would be because she decided to have sex with Keenan. And that, she told herself, opening the bathroom door, wasn't going to happen. Not only for her sake, but for his, as well.

Keenan passed her on his way to the bathroom. Mitzi noticed the pajamas Mrs. Thompsett had loaned him were still on the bed.

Mitzi scooped them into her arms. "Heads up."

He whirled and the blue pj's hit him in the face.

"Don't come out of that room without those on." Her tone held a warning edge.

Keenan grinned, lifted a hand in a mock salute. "Yes, ma'am."

HER KIND OF HERO | 121

Mitzi was propped in bed, reading a *Home and Garden* magazine she'd found on the bedside table, when Keenan returned several minutes later wearing the pajamas.

His towel-dried hair curled lightly above his collar. She caught a faint floral aroma as he strolled by with the clothes he'd been wearing in his hands.

"Love the new scent." Her smile widened when he turned and scowled. "Such a manly fragrance."

"All the soaps were the same," he told her, his tone filled with disgust. "Roses."

He placed his folded clothes atop the antique dresser inlaid with burl.

"I happen to like the scent."

"That makes one of us." He plucked at the two-sizes-too-large pajama pants he wore. "And these are a joke."

"Aren't we Mr. Cheerful?"

Rain hammered against the roof and a crack of too-close lightning shook the house.

Keenan's gaze jumped to her face. His tight expression eased into a smile. "You're right. I could be stretched out on cold concrete in the hangar."

"Wait until you feel the mattress." Mitzi patted the spot beside her. "Heavenly soft."

The look Keenan shot her was clearly puzzled. "I thought I'd grab a pillow and stretch out on the floor."

"Are you crazy? Why would you do that?"

His gaze searched her face. "You don't mind sharing the bed?"

"Not as long as I get my half."

Keenan didn't say another word. He flipped off the main light and hopped in beside her. The only light in the room came from a fussy bedside lamp that cast a golden glow.

Outside, thunder continued to rumble, but the torrent on the roof had turned soft and soothing.

It had been a long time since she'd slept with anyone, Mitzi realized. She and her sister had shared a bed for years. But once she'd moved away from home, she'd insisted on her own space.

She'd never slept all night with the men she dated. Having a man beside her all night had always seemed so...intimate.

When Keenan was in the shower, she'd decided it was time to break herself of the hang-up.

After punching the pillow several times, Keenan laid back and closed his eyes, his lashes dark against his cheeks.

Good, Mitzi thought, just as she hoped.

She flipped off the lamp, settled in beside him and slept.

Several hours later she awoke to find an arm flung over her and Keenan's hand resting over her breast. She started to slip out from under his hold, when his fingers began to tease her nipple into a peak.

His touch felt so good she couldn't bring herself to move away. Keenan continued to tease, to caress, even as his eyes remained closed.

Her nipples strained against the thin fabric, eager for the touch. When his hand moved to her other breast, she repositioned herself to give him better access. He turned her in his arms and kissed her long and hard. The flame in her belly began to burn, hot and filled with need.

"Keenan." She breathed his name.

He tugged at the hem of her gown. "Take this off."

Mitzi told herself to stop, to take a breath. To think. Was this what was best? Was this what she wanted? She wasn't sure about the answer to the first, but she was certain about the second.

She began unbuttoning the front of his pajama top, but he grew impatient and jerked it over his head. It hit the floor along with his pants only seconds later.

When he pulled her close, she felt him, long and hard against her belly.

His eyes were open now, dark and filled with need. "Are you sure?"

HER KIND OF HERO | 123

She chuckled. "Little late for that question."

"Are you sure?" he asked again.

Mitzi nodded. "You?"

"Yes," he said, not taking his eyes off hers.

"Even if it's just one night?"

"Yes." The palms of his hands moved up and down her body in slow, sensual strokes. "You're beautiful."

"You're beautiful, too," she whispered.

He had broad, well-muscled shoulders. She liked the way those muscles felt beneath her fingers, the way they rippled and responded. She couldn't remember the last time she'd wanted a man so desperately.

Though she didn't fully understand this intense need for him, it didn't change the fact that she had to have him.

His mouth closed over hers, the kiss sweet and gentle at first then heating up as his lips lingered. She reveled in the feel of that firm warm mouth against hers, in the taste of him.

The caresses continued even as he kissed her and drove her closer and closer to the edge with his skilled touch.

Her body burned and there was only one person who could quench the fire.

His touch was urgent, as if the same passion that burned inside her flowed through his veins. She cried out as the desire built to a fever crest, and he covered the sound with his mouth. With firm warm lips.

She wanted to crawl under his skin, anything to get closer to him.

"Are you protected?" she heard him ask, his voice tight with restraint.

"Yes." She managed to form the word before he drove himself into her.

Ah, yes, she thought through a haze of mounting desire, this was what she wanted. *He* was what she wanted.

The thought brought with it a flash of worry, but she brushed it aside. For now, there was just her and him. For now, nothing else mattered.

They made love two more times, then fell asleep, exhausted. She opened her eyes to sunlight streaming through the window and found him propped up on one elbow, staring, his hazel eyes dark and unreadable.

Then he smiled and warmth flowed through her veins like warm honey.

"Good morning." He touched her cheek lightly with one finger. "You look rested."

Sated was more accurate. Mitzi stretched like a contented cat, noting with interest that Keenan was still naked. How...convenient.

"Are you hungry?"

She found his voice, gravelly with recent sleep, incredibly sexy.

Mitzi had no doubt Mrs. Thompsett had a dining room table full of food waiting downstairs. But it wasn't food she wanted at this moment.

She leaned forward, brushed her lips across his and let the sheet fall to her waist. "I am. What are you going to do about it?"

Because she wasn't the only one starving, he pulled her to him.

They showered together, dressed and then went downstairs. In deference to Mitzi's reputation in the small community, Keenan made sure to keep his hands to himself.

It was a difficult task. He found himself wanting to touch her, to reassure himself that what had happened last night had been real and not a highly charged erotic dream. He wanted to convince himself that she had indeed wanted him as much as he'd wanted her.

HER KIND OF HERO | 125

They ate as if they hadn't had food in weeks, plowing their way through wedges of cherry-stuffed French toast and crisp bacon. Orange juice so tart it bit his tongue and coffee that packed a nice punch.

While his clothes were rumpled and disheveled, Mitzi looked like a princess holding court. Keenan admired her composure, the way she could appear so friendly, yet easily deflect any personal questions. Was this the real Mitzi?

Keenan was happy when Perry dropped them off at the airstrip with a friendly wave and he was alone with her again.

They found blue skies and calm winds for the trip back to Jackson. Steve had agreed with the decision to stay the night rather than fly back. And Joel, when Keenan had reached him this morning, had told him it was his choice to come in late or not at all today.

"Do you have to go into the clinic today?" Keenan asked in a nonchalant tone as they approached the parking lot of the airstrip outside of Jackson. "Or see patients at the hospital?"

"Actually, I've got the day off." While she spoke, her gaze remained focused on the inside of her purse as she rummaged around in search of her car keys.

"I'm going riding," he said. "Tripp's dad has been urging me to come out and give his horses some exercise. It looks like it's going to be a beautiful day. Interested in joining me?"

When she looked up and he caught her hesitation, Keenan offered an easy smile. "No strings. I simply thought you might enjoy doing something fun and out of the ordinary on your day off."

"It'd be out of the ordinary." Mitzi offered an impish smile. "And certainly an adventure, considering I've never ridden a horse."

"The way I see it, an adventurous woman would never turn down an opportunity to try something new." Keenan kept his tone light, prepared to go with the flow. "Are you in?"

126 | CINDY KIRK

"Saddle up that filly." Mitzi grinned. "This cowgirl is ready to ride."

~

Had she lost her mind?

Yes, Mitzi thought as she stepped from the shower, she had not only lost her mind, she kept losing it. Instead of pushing Keenan away, as any sensible woman would have done after a night of ill-advised mind-blowing sex, she'd compounded the error by spending the day with him.

Riding horses had been a blast, she admitted as she dried off then slathered on lotion. The sun had been bright, but there'd been a slight breeze that had kept her from getting too warm.

Keenan had kept the conversation light and innocuous. They talked sports and she discovered that, like her, he loved the slopes and preferred to ski the more challenging backcountry.

Though neither mentioned what had happened in Delano, the fire that had sizzled between them now burned hotter than ever. At least it did for her. When Keenan had extended his hand to help her mount the horse, the mere touch of his flesh against hers had brought an ache of wanting so intense it had stolen her breath.

If he experienced the same shock, it hadn't shown. A fact she found both reassuring and disturbing.

Then, as if spending the night and then the day with him hadn't been enough, she'd accepted Kathy Randall's invitation to return with Keenan that evening for a family dinner.

Of course, Tripp and Adrianna *were* part of the wide network of friends she'd socialized with since arriving in Jackson Hole. There was no reason to avoid them. And really, if she was being completely rational, no reason to avoid Keenan.

They'd had sex. So what? They were young and single. They'd had an itch and scratched it. End of story.

HER KIND OF HERO | 127

If the opportunity came up to do it again, there was nothing saying she wouldn't consider it. Since she and Keenan had reached an understanding, he'd probably be cool with it, too. Until she found someone she wanted to seriously date, she was as free as the wind.

The thought cheered her as she took her cowgirl shirt—poppy-red with pearl buttons and white piping around the pockets—from the closet. The jean skirt she planned to wear with it was already laid out on the bed.

Bitty jumped up onto the four-poster and headed straight for the skirt.

"No, no, Bitty." Mitzi grabbed the kitten and pulled her close, stroking the soft fur.

"There's nothing wrong with spending time with Keenan," she murmured to herself as Bitty looked up then raked her sandpaper tongue across the top of Mitzi's hand. "I just have to keep myself from liking him too much."

That shouldn't be a problem. Most men she'd dated accused her of having ice in her veins. Of course, they usually didn't hit her with that zinger until she'd broken it off. It was her practice that once she was ready to move on, to simply tell the guy. She would never understand the ones who kept calling, trying to get her to change her mind.

Ice in her veins? Though it seemed a trifle harsh, she could honestly admit there had never been a man she couldn't walk away from and none whom she missed once he was gone.

Mitzi thought of Devin, a fellow medical-school student. When they'd started going out, she'd made it clear she wasn't looking for anything serious. He seemed cool with the arrangement, but sometime during the year he apparently changed his mind.

When he'd professed his love and pulled out a diamond ring, she'd been struck dumb. Though she'd attempted to be gentle in her refusal, he'd become angry. Looking back, she accepted some of the fault for that...misunderstanding. She should have never let such long stretches go by without reminding Devin they were just friends. She certainly never should have let dating turn into an exclusive arrangement.

While she may have made it clear at the beginning of the relationship she only wanted to be friends, she hadn't been vigilant during the course of their time together.

Mitzi wouldn't make the same mistake with Keenan. She'd be alert for any signs that he might be getting the wrong idea about their "friendship."

The doorbell rang and Mitzi scrambled to her feet. She took a moment to dress, tug on her boots and freshen her lipstick before sashaying to the front door to greet Keenan.

Keenan couldn't remember the last time he'd laughed so much. After a dinner of barbecued brisket with Kathy Randall's peach pie for dessert, he and Mitzi gave in to pressure and agreed to a game of charades.

Keenan smiled. Bill and the other married guys he worked with were always teasing him about his "wild" single life. He could only imagine what they'd think if he told them he'd followed an evening of playing cards with a hot night of charades.

Hailey ran the game, which pitted girls against guys. Keenan, Tripp and Frank were on one team with Adrianna, Mitzi and Kathy on the other. The teams were evenly matched with each enjoying its share of success.

"We won!" Mitzi shrieked at Adrianna's correct answer and pumped her fist in the air. Kathy and Adrianna exchanged high fives and shot smug smiles to the men.

Frank turned to his son, looking disgusted. "We should have

HER KIND OF HERO | 129

gotten that last point. I don't know how I could have made the clues any more obvious."

Tripp shrugged. "Can't win 'em all."

But Keenan could tell Tripp was as upset by the loss as his father. It was easy to see where his friend had inherited his competitive streak.

Tripp helped his wife up from the sofa. While her pregnancy didn't show, his friend had been overly solicitous all evening. "We're going to call it a night. Adrianna and I have early appointments tomorrow."

"Likewise." Mitzi rose. "My schedule the next few days is murderous."

Keenan helped Tripp and Frank rearrange the furniture that had been scooted together for the game. He kept his face impassive, wondering if Mitzi's words had been for his benefit. Was that her way of telling him not to call, not to expect to see her for the next few days?

She needn't have wasted her breath. Keenan had no intention of running after her. Even when he was a boy, he hadn't chased girls. They'd come to him.

Or...they hadn't.

Keenan had enjoyed the evening. The only downer was the loving way Tripp and Hailey interacted with their mother brought some not-so-fond memories of his own mother to the surface.

But he *had* gotten something of value from living in her household. Gloria had taught him—through words and example —that if he put his heart out there, it'd get stomped on. She'd stomped on his repeatedly until he smartened up and realized she didn't care. Not about Betsy. Not about him.

It had been a valuable lesson. One he needed to keep in mind, especially where the capricious Dr. Sanchez was concerned.

CHAPTER FOURTEEN

Though Mitzi informed Keenan she was perfectly capable of walking from the car to her porch, he insisted on accompanying her to the front door.

She wondered if he expected her to invite him in. If that was his plan, he was setting the stage properly, acting friendly but cool since leaving the Randall ranch. But she saw the desire in his eyes and wasn't fooled. The fact that he smelled terrific wasn't going to change her mind, either.

But she *had* reconsidered her earlier decision to forgo a goodnight kiss. What harm would there be in two friends exchanging a kiss at the door?

The air had taken on a slight chill, but Mitzi reveled in the breeze against her warm cheeks. Just having Keenan so close in the car, inhaling the intoxicating scent of his cologne, remembering the way his body had fit so perfectly against hers, had set her blood to boiling.

Just one little kiss, she decided. To take the edge off.

She shoved the key into the new lock with fingers that trembled slightly, her heart already beginning to race with anticipation. The man certainly knew how to kiss. And the things he could do with his tongue.

Her knees went weak, remembering.

Yet when she turned back to Keenan, she found him a good two feet away.

He smiled, flashed those straight white teeth in an easy grin. "I had fun tonight."

She paused, suddenly unsteady. It was as if she'd known exactly where she was headed, only to have him change the path at the last second.

"I did, too. I'd never played charades before." Her gaze dropped from his eyes to his lips. Dear God, could she be any more obvious?

"You're smart." He shoved his hands into his pockets, rocked back on his heels. "Intelligent people excel at charades."

Mitzi didn't feel smart now. She wanted him to kiss her, but obviously she wasn't making her feelings clear. Still, how much more obvious could she be? Grabbing his shirt and pulling him to her seemed a bit dramatic, especially when all she wanted was a simple peck on the lips.

As her frustration soared, Mitzi acknowledged a peck on the lips wasn't going to cut it tonight. She wanted one of the kisses from last night, the kind where their mouths fused, where his tongue slipped past her lips and stroked, reminding her of what he'd felt like inside her.

To her horror, she felt herself go damp as an ache of longing settled between her thighs.

"Stay for a—" she found herself saying, but it was too late.

Keenan was already pulling his car door open, then offering a careless wave as he backed out.

Mitzi could only plaster a smile on her lips, lift a hand in goodbye...and yearn for the kiss she hadn't received.

∼

132 | CINDY KIRK

The next few days were so busy there wasn't time for Mitzi to dwell on the fact that Keenan hadn't kissed her good-night. By the time she got home, the workmen—including Keenan—had gone. Only Bitty was there to greet her.

This Saturday was her day to give something back to the community that had become her home. Mitzi and the other doctors in the practice had volunteered to work brief shifts in the medical tent at a local "Harvest Fun Run." Anticipating sprained ankles and injured knees, she almost swallowed her tongue when Keenan walked in with Joel and Gabe. All sported multiple stings. A hornet's nest, hidden in a large tree not far from the starting line, had fallen.

Thankfully the three had arrived late and were the only runners affected.

As two PAs assessed Joel and Gabe, Mitzi took care of Keenan. His handsome face had several stings but his arms exhibited the most welts.

For the first few minutes, she was all doctor—getting his allergy history, checking for signs of respiratory distress, cleaning an oily residue from his arm and face before removing remaining stingers with the flat edge of a scalpel.

Mitzi knew hornet stings contained acetylcholine, a neuro-transmitter that helped transmit pain signals to the brain. Surprisingly, Keenan didn't seem that uncomfortable. She gently placed an ice pack on his arm. "On a scale of one to ten, where would you place your current pain level, if one is no pain and ten is the worst?"

"Right now it's a four." Keenan repositioned himself on the bench, winced when his arm shifted beneath the ice pack. "It was close to a seven when we ran into Bill on our way here. He got some WD-40 out of his truck and sprayed the areas where we were stung."

Mitzi had heard of the folk remedy but had never known

HER KIND OF HERO | 133

anyone who'd used it. "I wondered about the oily substance on your arm."

"It sounded weird to me," Keenan said with a sheepish grin. "When Bill said his granny swore by it, we decided to give it a try."

"Well, the home remedy appears to have worked." Mitzi smiled and gently repositioned the ice bag.

"You have good hands."

When she looked up, her gaze met his. Memories flooded back. A cozy room. Rain pitter-pattering on the roof. The feel of Keenan's warm flesh against her...

"I'm not the only one. You have good hands, too," she murmured in a low tone.

His lips quirked in a grin and she basked in the warmth of his smile.

They'd shared so much. In the short time she'd known him, Mitzi had come to consider Keenan a close friend. She thought she knew everything there was to know about him. Today had shown her she'd been wrong. "I didn't realize you were a runner."

"I'm not." He shrugged. "Stone Craft is one of the sponsors. Joel thought it was important we participate. I thought it'd be fun. I didn't count on hornets making an appearance."

"What are you doing this evening—?" she impulsively began.

"Keenan." Gabe paused at the entrance of the tent. "Joel and I aren't about to let a few oversized wasps keep us down. We're going to finish the race. You coming?"

"You bet." Keenan rose, gave Mitzi's shoulder a squeeze. "Thanks, Doc. I'll be seeing you."

"Yeah," Mitzi managed to mumble. "I'll see you around."

"Wow," one of the nurses said to Mitzi as Keenan strode out. "He sure is hot. Who is he?"

Keenan disappeared from view and Mitzi resisted the urge to sigh. "A friend. A good friend."

134 | CINDY KIRK

~

On Sunday, Keenan dressed for church and told himself he'd done the right thing by keeping his distance from Mitzi. Though he'd accepted her apology and she seemed to enjoy riding horses with him, during the evening at the Randall ranch he'd sensed her distancing herself from him. Keenan got the feeling if he pushed for more closeness, she'd pull all the way back.

That he wouldn't allow to occur. While he might not be looking for anything serious—and she'd made it perfectly clear she sure as heck wasn't—he didn't want her to break all ties. So he was giving her breathing room, time to realize she wasn't the only one committed to keeping things light.

Yet, every night when five o'clock rolled around, he hadn't been able to stop himself from lingering just a little longer than everyone else, hoping to run into her.

Having their paths cross in the medical tent at the race had been a stroke of good luck. It had been an extra bonus that she'd been the one to tend to his wounds.

Her touch had been gentle, her eyes filled with such compassion, he'd been tempted to ask if he could buy her dinner as a gesture of thanks. But wariness still lurked in those blue depths, so he'd kept his mouth shut.

He paused at the stoplight several blocks from the church and gazed down at the brown pants and the cream-colored shirt he'd picked up at the big-box store where he and Mitzi had once "shopped" for samples.

Betsy had urged him to come to church today, told him she missed seeing him. How could he refuse?

He'd already agreed when she mentioned going out for breakfast after the service. Apparently Sunday breakfast at The Coffee Pot was practically a tradition among their group of friends.

Is Mitzi part of the group that meets? he wanted to ask, but kept his mouth shut. Though he didn't like keeping things from his

HER KIND OF HERO | 135

sister and her husband—who was one of his closest friends—neither did he want them speculating about his relationship with Mitzi.

He and Mitzi didn't have a relationship. They were simply friends.

Friends who'd slept together.

The sex had exceeded his wildest expectations. Of course, because he'd been celibate for the past three years, any sex might seem phenomenal. Keenan suspected it had been so extraordinary because of the connection he and Mitzi shared. Though he wasn't about to put his heart out there to get stomped on, he liked knowing he was capable of feeling close to someone.

By the time Keenan parked and entered the small white church, everyone was standing for the first hymn. He glanced over the crowd but couldn't pick out Betsy and Ryan. For a brief moment, he considered grabbing a seat in the back until he saw the last three or four pews held parents and their young children.

The next couple of rows were filled with teenagers. Even if there had been room, no way was Keenan sitting there. Thankfully he noticed what appeared to be a single space at the end of a pew halfway down the aisle. As the congregation headed into the final refrain, Keenan made a dash and slipped into the space.

The smile he'd placed on his face froze when Mitzi turned. Her eyes widened and she juggled the hymnal in her hands. On the other side of her sat Adrianna and Tripp.

Tripp nodded and smiled and Adrianna mouthed a welcome. But Keenan couldn't keep his eyes off Mitzi. "What a nice surprise."

"I didn't know you went to church here," she whispered.

"I don't," he responded in an equally low tone. "Betsy texted me last night—"

An older woman in front of him turned and fixed her sharp-eyed gaze on him. Though it had been fifteen years, Keenan recognized the winged, silver-rimmed glasses and no-nonsense expression. It was Mrs. Applebee, his biology teacher in eleventh grade. "Shh."

It wasn't a warning, but a command.

Beside him, Mitzi chuckled, but Keenan wasn't so cavalier. He'd had plenty of experience being on the bad side of this specific teacher's wrath. Feeling sixteen again, he fixed his gaze on the hymnal and shut his mouth.

The service went quickly. The building was familiar, the inside not so much. He'd dropped Betsy off here every Sunday when she was growing up. Gloria always partied extra hard on Saturday nights and often had men sleep over. The way he saw it, the less his sister was exposed to Gloria and her hungover friends, the better.

While Bets was doing the Sunday-school thing, he'd shoot baskets at the elementary school just down the road. The only time Keenan had gone to church was if Betsy had been in a program. He'd felt it important she had family in the audience.

Whenever Gloria had been on the wagon, she'd come along. Keenan could count that number of times on one hand.

He pulled his thoughts back to the present as everyone rose for the closing hymn. By the time the song ended and the minister did the benediction, he still hadn't spotted his sister. The phone in his pocket buzzed just as the service ended.

Though he wanted to pull it out and check for a text, Keenan wasn't sure of the proper protocol while in the sanctuary. Was it okay to check and send texts? Read email?

It seemed as if it should be. After all, it wasn't as if he'd be talking on the phone and disturbing those around him. Mrs. Applebee's earlier censuring gaze told Keenan he'd be taking a risk by pulling out the phone.

"I didn't expect to see you here." Tripp leaned around Adrianna to shake his hand. "Glad you came."

"Betsy asked if I'd meet her and Ryan this morning." Keenan's

HER KIND OF HERO | 137

gaze scoured the faces streaming down the aisle. "Have you seen them?"

"I haven't," Tripp said.

Adrianna and Mitzi looked at each other then shook their heads.

"Ryan never came to church before Betsy," Adrianna commented. "He'd simply show up at The Coffee Pot for breakfast."

Mitzi's nod confirmed the fact.

"Betsy did say something about getting together for breakfast." Keenan rubbed his chin.

"Join us." Tripp clapped Keenan on the back. "Try the Western omelet. Can't be beat."

Fifteen minutes later, Keenan found himself at a back table surrounded by longtime friends. Mitzi chose a seat across from him, rather than by his side. That was okay. His position gave him a good view of the front door. This way he could easily spot Betsy and Ryan.

There were several empty seats at the end of the table and each time the doorbell jingled, Keenan looked up to see if it was his sister. By the time everyone had ordered and Betsy and Ryan still hadn't showed up, Keenan texted her.

Her reply came swiftly back. He frowned.

"I hope nothing is wrong," Mitzi murmured.

"They forgot about meeting me." Keenan read the text again then shoved the phone back into his pocket. "Nate is throwing up."

"Gastroenteritis is going around," Kate tossed out, reminding him there were no private conversations at the table. "Our waiting room was full all week."

"He's so small." Keenan thought of the toddler with the fearless grin.

The pediatrician reached over and gave Keenan's hand a slight

138 | CINDY KIRK

squeeze. "Your nephew should weather this illness without any problem. He's a strong, healthy boy."

"And Betsy is a good mother," he heard Mary Karen Fisher say.

If anyone should know mothering, it was MK. A nurse with five little ones, she somehow managed to always look as if she didn't have a care in the world.

"It's amazing how good Betsy is with Nathan." Keenan lifted his coffee mug, thought of Gloria. "Considering she had such a poor example to follow."

"My parents weren't very demonstrative affection-wise," Adrianna said softly. "I'm determined to be more openly affectionate with our little one."

Tripp looped an arm around his wife's shoulder. "You'll be a fantastic mother."

"Being a parent is a demanding job," Benedict said from across the table, his hand curved around his wife's. Seated in an infant seat in the chair next to her, their baby boy slept, dressed in a white-and-blue sailor outfit. "But a rewarding one."

"Is anyone else going to participate in the Jaycees' 'Go Blue for a Cure?'" Though Mitzi's comment may have appeared to come out of left field, there was only so much talk about babies she could take.

"Go Blue for a Cure?" Adrianna pulled her brows together, her emerald eyes puzzled.

"Cassidy mentioned it at the last Jackson After-Hours event," Lexi, a local social worker with a dark chin-length bob, interjected. "She mentioned it again when the girls and I stopped by her salon a few days ago for haircuts."

"I'm as clueless as Adrianna," Winn said, shooting the nurse midwife a charming smile.

Mitzi had been relieved that Winn had taken a seat at the other end of the table. Apparently she wasn't the only one who realized they weren't a good fit.

HER KIND OF HERO | 139

"It's a fund-raiser," Mitzi said, when no one jumped in to answer. The purpose was near and dear to an orthopedic surgeon's heart. "The majority of the money will go to fund osteogenic sarcoma research. A portion will go to Ariela Svehla's parents to help with her medical expenses."

Last month Mitzi had been forced to amputate the girl's left leg midthigh in an attempt to eradicate the cancer that threatened her young life.

"Ariela's father is a bricklayer with Stone Craft." Sympathy filled Keenan's eyes. "Nice guy."

"The way it works is participants get people—sponsors—to donate money," Mitzi continued. "For those donations, participants are required to color or highlight their hair some shade of blue."

"An excuse to be wild and crazy." Tripp grinned. "Count me in."

"How often do we get the opportunity as adults to do something like this?" Lexi's husband, Nick, was a prominent attorney with a large family law practice in both Jackson Hole and Dallas. In recent years, he and Lexi spent more time in Jackson Hole, with him commuting whenever necessary.

"Don't tell me you're going to dye your hair blue, Delacourt." Winn sounded shocked. "Your high-profile clients will hardly appreciate seeing the man they chose to represent them looking like some punk rocker."

Nick laughed good-naturedly. "They'll understand, once I tell them the reason. I might even get more sponsors."

Sensing Nick had made up his mind, Winn turned to Mitzi. "You're going to do it?"

"Absolutely," Mitzi responded without hesitation.

"Well, count me out." Winn straightened his Hermès tie. "I am, however, willing to make a sizable donation to the cause."

Mitzi reached down, grabbed a sponsor sheet from her purse

and shoved it in front of him. "Put your money where your mouth is, Ferris."

Looking pained, Winn pulled out his Montblanc.

Once the breakfast ended, those who didn't have to run to the church to pick up kids stood talking outside the café. It was as if, Mitzi thought, they were reluctant to leave behind the friendship and camaraderie they'd enjoyed inside.

Winn rushed off, mentioning an important conference call. Mitzi wondered if it was an excuse. Perhaps he thought she'd attempt to convince him that blue was his color. Her lips curved up in a smile. The guy really needed to loosen up.

"What kind of person sets up a conference call for Sunday morning?" someone asked.

"I'm thinking he was afraid." Mitzi tossed her head, a sly smile on her lips. "Afraid I'd convince him to go blue."

"You've got to give the guy credit." Keenan chuckled and rubbed his chin. "He recognizes the power of Mitzi."

CHAPTER FIFTEEN

Since they'd parked in the same vicinity, it seemed natural for Mitzi to fall into step beside Keenan when the group dispersed.

"Got big plans for the day?" She kept her tone conversational, one friend to another.

"Thought I'd head over to Yellowstone. We won't get many more days like this." His gaze lifted to the clear blue sky before dropping to fix on her. "Ryan mentioned last week I could borrow his kayak. With Nate sick, he and Betsy won't be using it today."

He reached around her and opened the car door she'd just unlocked. "You should come with me."

Mitzi started to say no, but stopped herself. A friend had invited her to do something she enjoyed on her day off. Why was she hesitating? If their friendship stood any chance of flourishing, she had to quit being so hypervigilant. And there was no better time to start than now.

Hours later, when the bright afternoon sun had begun to droop, Mitzi helped Keenan load the kayak back on the top of the ancient Explorer they'd borrowed from Ryan and Betsy.

Accepting the invitation had been the right decision. They

were just two buds enjoying the great outdoors. Laughing. Talking. Splashing. Simple pleasures.

Mitzi took a long sip of water as her "buddy" secured the last strap around the bright orange boat. From the smile on Keenan's lips, he'd enjoyed the day, too.

After spending most of her life needing to be the one in charge, it had been surprisingly pleasant to sit back and let Keenan steer them expertly around boulders and a few heart-thumping logjams.

"I never thought anything named Bitch Creek could be so beautiful," she said, thinking of the breathtaking basalt canyon they'd floated through this afternoon.

"I'm glad the route worked out." Keenan raked a hand through damp hair, reminding her how he looked when he'd stepped out of the shower at the B and B. Ruggedly handsome. All male. "Normally at this time of year it's too shallow to negotiate. The creek is fed by runoff."

"You know your way around a kayak." Mitzi cast him an admiring glance before taking another long pull from the water bottle.

When she noticed him watching her, she thrust the bottle in his direction. "Be my guest."

Keenan drained the rest in one gulp. When he caught her staring, he grinned sheepishly. "I was thirsty."

"I'd never have guessed." Even as Mitzi spoke, her gaze dropped back to his mouth. All afternoon she'd done her best to keep her focus off those talented lips. Now she couldn't seem to tear her gaze away.

His smile faded. An arousing intensity replaced the teasing glint in his eyes.

Keep it light, Mitzi told herself. "I was wondering if you'd mind stopping at the store when we get back into town."

He blinked. "Store?"

"The market." She would.not.look.at.his.lips. "I need to pick up a few things for the coming week."

"Sure." He rocked back on his heels. "No problem."

After stowing the Explorer and the kayak back in his sister's garage, they dropped his Impala off in front of the boardinghouse. The spark of pleasure in his eyes when she tossed him the keys to the BMW made Mitzi glad she'd made the gesture.

On the edge of town, Keenan pulled into the parking lot of the grocery store he'd frequented as a kid. Though he hadn't been interested in going to the market, neither had he been ready for this day with Mitzi to end.

When they'd dropped off his car and she'd tossed him the keys to hers, he knew she was inviting him to spend the night. Since he'd be working tomorrow at her place, he didn't need his vehicle.

"This shouldn't take long," Mitzi told him as the automatic doors at the front of the store slid open.

"I'm in no hurry." It felt natural to walk beside her, to stroll up and down the aisles with her while she grabbed milk, yogurt and a carton of eggs. Natural to talk and joke with the older woman standing behind them as they waited in the checkout lane. Natural to simply be with Mitzi.

Twenty minutes later, Keenan walked out into the warm evening air, a sack of groceries in one arm and the most beautiful woman in Jackson Hole at his side. Life didn't get much better.

"Dr. Sanchez?"

The feminine voice had them both turning. Keenan didn't recognize the middle-aged woman with the tightly curled hair and silver-rimmed glasses, but Mitzi's smile widened. She greeted the woman by name.

After Mitzi performed introductions, Keenan stepped back,

listening while the woman updated the doctor on her husband's "amazing" postsurgical progress.

Before the woman interrupted, Keenan had found himself thinking how easily he could get used to this being his life—doing fun activities with Mitzi as well as enjoying the day-to-day. It was just a pipe dream.

Mitzi had made it very clear—and had continued to make it clear—what she wanted and didn't want in a man, what she expected and didn't expect from him specifically. His focus needed to be on his own future. Until he reached the goals he'd set, he had little to offer the successful doctor.

Nothing...except his heart.

And he'd learned long ago, that wasn't worth much.

"Got it. Five-thirty. Clippety Do-Dah," Mitzi said into the phone, a lilt lifting her voice. "See you then."

Ben looked up from the file of the patient they'd been discussing until Mitzi had silenced him with a wave of one hand to answer her phone. He raised a brow. "*That* was your important call?"

She grinned. "Keenan and I are getting our hair dyed blue on Thursday."

Her colleague shook his head, a bemused look on his face. "You're really going through with it?"

"I have over a thousand dollars in pledges riding on going through with it." Mitzi waved a hand. "No backing out now. Actually, I'm jazzed about the opportunity to go crazy with color and support a good cause at the same time."

"What about Keenan?"

"Last I knew he hadn't hit a thousand yet." Mitzi pulled her brows together, tried to recall his last update. "More like seven hundred fifty."

Ben opened his mouth. Shut it. He glanced down at the file and focused on the patient. Ten minutes of discussion later, Mitzi rose to leave.

"One more thing." Ben motioned her back. "I noticed you and Keenan have been spending a lot of time together."

"We're friends." Mitzi spoke cautiously, wondering just where Ben was headed. Normally he gave her personal life a wide berth.

"I've also noticed you've been in a much better mood since he became your 'friend.'"

Was that really a teasing gleam in her colleague's eyes? Couldn't be. Ben wasn't the teasing type. He was serious. Too serious. Too cerebral.

"Keenan knows how to enjoy life." She thought of the rock climbing he'd urged her to try. "He's very physical."

When Ben's grin widened, she gave his arm a punch. "I meant Keenan likes physical activities—"

Though Mitzi didn't believe it was possible, Ben's grin inched even wider.

"Kayaking, windsurfing, horseback riding." She ticked them off her fingers one by one.

"I'm just saying the guy has been good for you," Ben said equitably.

Mitzi shifted, uncomfortable at the direction of the conversation. Ben wasn't the first to assume she and Keenan were a couple. Considering they spent so much time together, she supposed it was understandable.

Heck, they'd even gone to church together the past two Sundays. And she couldn't immediately recall the last time she'd slept alone. Still, she'd made sure to mention numerous times what his *friendship* meant to her. Each time, he'd smile and call her "buddy."

She had to admit she kind of liked the way the word sounded on his tongue.

"It's important to have friends you feel comfortable with,

146 | CINDY KIRK

whose company you enjoy." Ben met her gaze. "You and I, we were never really friends."

Mitzi pushed back from the office chair and stood. She and Ben had never discussed what had gone wrong between them. The way she recalled it, they'd simply argued one too many times and neither cared enough to try to repair the damage of the angry words.

Though they shared a love of practicing medicine, they'd taken vastly different routes to arrive at where they were now. Ben could no more understand what drove her than she could understand what drove him.

"Even from the beginning there was this ease, this comfort, with Poppy." Ben's eyes darkened with emotion. "It was never easy between us."

"You always were master of the understatement, Benedict." Mitzi stifled a snort. "It was like riding a roller coaster. A few wild peaks. A whole lot of valleys."

"Poppy and I enjoy quiet evenings together." Ben rubbed his chin. "You had to always go out."

Mitzi started to deny it then realized he spoke the truth. The thought of spending an evening alone with Ben watching a movie and sharing a bowl of popcorn had never held any appeal.

The fact that he'd been willing to escort her to all the social events in Jackson Hole—and she'd discovered since moving here there was always something to do—had probably prolonged their relationship long after it should have come to an end.

"I've actually discovered I can stay home and enjoy watching movies." Mitzi thought of the scary horror flick she and Keenan had seen the other night. She'd even had to close her eyes at one point. Keenan had laughed. But when he'd wrapped his arms around her, she hadn't been scared anymore. "In moderate doses, even cards and charades can be fun."

"Charades?"

Mitzi smiled at the shock Ben infused in that single word.

"I'm glad we didn't attempt to hang on to something that wasn't working," Ben said. "I think we've both found something far better."

"Are you seeing your *friend* tonight?" Bill asked Keenan, before turning to load some tools into the back of his pickup.

Keenan wiped the sweat from his brow with the back of his hand. "As a matter of fact I'm going to a *quinceañera* with Mitzi this evening."

Bill rested his back against his red pickup that gleamed in the sunlight and tilted his head. "A what?"

"I asked the same thing," Keenan admitted. "It's a party thrown when a girl turns fifteen."

Bill lifted a brow. "Like a birthday party?"

"I guess." Keenan shrugged. "But a bigger deal."

"Who's it for? Anyone I know?"

"Mitzi's office billing manager, Consuela Herrera. The party is for her daughter."

"You're moving up in the world, boy." Bill slapped Keenan on the back. "From the slammer to escorting one of the most eligible doctors in Jackson Hole to fancy parties in the span of a few short months."

Teasing or not, Bill's words served as a reminder just how far apart his and Mitzi's lives were and reinforced the importance of not getting too comfortable. Even if it sometimes felt like a whole lot more, he and Mitzi were simply friends. She reminded him of that fact constantly. Only a fool wouldn't take the warning to heart.

"Mitzi and I are just friends," he told Bill for what felt like the thousandth time.

"Look at these lines." Bill pointed to his drooping face. "Proof

I wasn't born yesterday. I've seen the way you look at her. And how she looks at you."

Keenan opened his mouth but Bill cut him off with a swipe of hand through the air.

"If I learned anything during my almost sixty years on this planet, it's that love don't come 'round all that often. When it does, you have to grab hold of it and not let go." Bill paused, gazed speculatively at Keenan. "You didn't survive those years in the Big House by being lily-livered. Be bold. Be brave. You know what you need to do."

CHAPTER SIXTEEN

Mitzi had told Keenan he needed to dress up for the *quinceañera* but wasn't sure what he'd show up wearing until he knocked and she opened the door.

Her heart stumbled. "Wow. You look terrific."

"Back at you." Keenan gazed admiringly at the simple navy dress she'd paired with a strand of pearls. She'd pulled her hair up and caught it in a glittery broach. "Too bad your hair isn't blue yet. Would have gone well with the dress."

"I thought that, too." Mitzi gave a little laugh before she ushered him inside, her fingers lingering on the fine fabric of his charcoal-gray suit. "This is nice."

"It's Ryan's," Keenan confessed. "When I told Bets I was going to this thing and needed to dress up, she gave me one of his to wear. He tossed in a shirt, tie and even the shoes."

"That was nice of him." Though Mitzi had never been physically attracted to Ryan, she considered him a friend. It was a shame she and Betsy had gotten off on the wrong foot. Maybe it was time to reach out to Keenan's sister.

"We better get going." She picked up the clutch on top of the sofa next to where the kitten now slept. She gave the soft top of Bitty's head a scratch. "Later, little one."

"She's content," Keenan observed.

"Why wouldn't she be?" Mitzi chuckled. Though she'd initially worried about taking on a pet because of the responsibility, Bitty had ended up being a nice addition to her household. "I give her everything she wants. That kitten has me wrapped around her little paw."

"You're a good person, Mitzi," Keenan said, surprising her. "Warm. Loving. Kind."

Heat stole up her neck and pleasure flowed like warm honey through her veins. She couldn't recall ever getting such a nice compliment. "One of my old boyfriends called me 'The Ice Queen.'"

"He must not have known you at all." Keenan opened the door for her and she inhaled the familiar soap and woodsy smell she'd come to associate with him.

"We can take my car tonight." Mitzi tossed him the keys.

"Second time in a week." He snagged the ring of keys midair. "What's the occasion?"

"It's muggy this evening."

"Just because Bertha's AC is on the fritz..." Keenan gave the Impala's fender a tap as he walked past. "She can't help it. She's old and ugly. Now, this baby..."

Keenan's gaze landed on Mitzi's BMW and he smiled. "Beautiful."

"More beautiful than me?" Mitzi couldn't believe she'd allowed the question to slip past her lips. Dr. Mitzi Sanchez didn't beg for compliments.

She braced herself for the slap down, a pithy one-liner that would make her feel even more foolish. Kelvin had been king of pithy one-liners. Especially if he sensed weakness.

Instead Keenan's eyes softened. She couldn't begin to describe

HER KIND OF HERO | 151

the look that filled them, but it made her feel warm and gooey inside.

"There's nothing and certainly no one more beautiful than you." He brought her hand to his lips. With his eyes still firmly focused on her, Keenan brushed a strand of hair back from her face. "Tonight you look especially delectable."

Just like that, Mitzi's confidence was back and she was ready to face the evening. She and Keenan chatted easily during the drive to the social hall.

After spending most of her working hours around people who were superintense, it was refreshing to simply enjoy the evening with a man who found humor in the most unlikely things and who didn't take himself or anyone else too seriously.

A good friend.

She thought about telling him—it never hurt to reinforce what they were to each other—but the conversation veered toward her house and when it would be completed.

"Another two weeks and you should be able to move the rest of your stuff in."

"We'll have to have a big party to celebrate." Mitzi stifled a groan as what she'd said registered. *We.* Had she really said *we?*

Keenan didn't appear to notice. "You definitely should show it off. Just make sure Bitty is locked in a bedroom. Having all those people around will freak her out."

"She's fine around you."

"She's used to me," he reminded her. "Sees me all day and most nights."

"True enough." Perhaps the knowledge should have disturbed her but it didn't.

"Tell me more about this shindig." He turned in the direction of the community hall in downtown Jackson.

"It's a big deal. Angela—Consuela's daughter—will be wearing a formal gown and the boys will be wearing tuxedos."

Keenan shifted in his seat when they stopped for a red light. "Seriously?"

"Like I said, it's a big deal."

He cast a questioning glance in her direction. "Did you have one of these things?"

"There was no money," Mitzi said simply. The year she turned fifteen, her eighteen-year-old sister had been pregnant with baby number two.

Keenan nodded and she saw he understood. It didn't surprise her. Sometimes she swore he could not only read her mind but see deep into her soul.

"Were we supposed to bring a gift?" he asked.

Mitzi wasn't sure if it made her feel better or not to hear Keenan use the plural. She tapped the clutch on her lap with her index finger. "In here."

"Must be small." Keenan looked mildly curious. "What is it?"

"A necklace. A silver cross with a blue topaz in the center."

"Sounds nice."

"When I was telling Consuela about my upcoming hair color change, she told me Angela's favorite color is blue." Mitzi lifted one shoulder. "I probably went a bit overboard. Blue topaz is my favorite stone and the art deco scrollwork on the cross caught my eye."

Mitzi realized she was babbling again, though she wasn't sure why. It wasn't a crime to buy someone a nice gift, the kind of gift she'd have killed to have gotten if there'd been money for her *quinceañera*.

Keenan pulled the car into the gravel parking lot next to the large frame building, making sure to avoid a couple of ruts the size of moon craters. "Is jewelry the gift of choice?"

"That or a Bible, prayer book or rosary." Mitzi's lips curved. "When I was that age I wanted anything with a blue stone. I'd also have accepted a tiara."

HER KIND OF HERO | 153

He shot her a teasing look, gave an exaggerated sigh. "A princess even back then."

Mitzi fingers curved around his hand as she stepped from the car. "A princess with no prince, no crown and no money."

He flashed a grin. "You don't want much."

She met his gaze. "I want it all."

"You deserve it all."

For some reason, instead of making her smile, her heart swelled with emotion. She'd never had anyone accept her so fully. Not even her own mother. She shifted her gaze and rapidly blinked away tears.

He held her arm as they negotiated the gravel lot. When they drew close to the entrance, Mitzi tugged him to a stop. "We need to talk about something."

"Okay." Looking suddenly ill at ease, Keenan slid his hands into his pockets. "Talk."

"The people who will be attending this event likely are most comfortable speaking Spanish. I know some think if they're in the United States they should speak English but—"

He touched her lips with the pad of one finger. "As far as I'm concerned, this is their party. They can speak Portuguese if they want. And, as long as there's cake, I'm happy."

"Trust me. There'll be cake." Still, she was glad she'd warned him because they were greeted in Spanish at the door.

Mitzi responded easily in her native tongue. Until she'd gone to kindergarten, Spanish was all she'd known. There had been a time as a young teen that she'd been embarrassed by her Mexican heritage. Now she was grateful. Being bilingual came in handy for patients with limited English.

Hector and Consuela spoke rapidly, expressing pleasure at her presence at their daughter's special day. Conscious of Keenan standing patiently at her side, Mitzi began the introductions.

Keenan extended his hand to Mr. Herrera and introduced himself in Spanish.

One more surprise from a man who seemed to constantly surprise her.

Consuela shot Mitzi an approving glance. "He will be your husband. He is why you needed a bigger home."

Mitzi saw the amusement in Keenan's eyes. She patted his arm. "He's my good friend."

"He will make a handsome husband." Consuela spoke as if they were alone, as if Keenan wasn't standing right there beside them with those laughing eyes understanding every word.

As soon as she could slip away, Mitzi tugged Keenan through a pink-and-white balloon arch into a hall sporting congratulatory banners and even more colored balloons.

"Looks like we got here just in time." Mitzi looped her arm through Keenan and pointed.

His gaze fixed on the group of young teenagers, currently positioning themselves in the center of the hardwood.

"The dance they'll perform is considered part of the celebration," Mitzi informed him. "It's usually well practiced and quite impressive."

"Can't be as impressive as that cake." Keenan let out a low whistle, gesturing with his head to a long table with a mound of presents at one end and a multitiered cake at the other.

"Angela's gift." Mitzi snapped open her purse, pulled out the box with shiny silver-and-white paper. "I'll be right back."

Leaving him where he stood, Mitzi hurried to the table and placed the gift where it wouldn't be lost or knocked aside. She returned to Keenan's side.

"I never asked the purpose of all this," he said as the choreographed dance of Angela and her "court" began.

"The *quinceañera* marks a girl's transition from childhood to maturity." Mitzi's heart swelled at the youthful innocence on the faces of the girls. "It celebrates the virtues of family, religion and social responsibilities."

The dance ended to bows and cheers, and Mitzi and Keenan joined in the applause.

They stayed at the party until after the toast and the presentation of the gifts. Before they left, Mitzi signed the guest book then took a moment to extend her congratulations and best wishes to Angela and her parents.

As they were walking out the door, Mitzi realized Keenan hadn't once pressed to leave. He'd laughed and talked with Consuela's family and friends. Over the course of the evening, he'd impressed them. And her.

Once they reached the car, Mitzi wound her arms around his neck. She pressed her mouth to his. "Thanks. I owe you."

Puzzlement filled his eyes. "For what?"

"For being a good sport."

He didn't say anything until they were in the car and heading down the road. "I'm not sure why you think you owe me. I enjoyed the evening."

Mitzi raised a skeptical brow.

"I enjoyed dancing with you." A rarely seen dimple in his right cheek flashed. "And the cake was excellent."

"Ah, yes, can't forget the cake."

"Most of all—" he reached over and took her hand "—I loved spending the evening with you."

When Keenan arrived on his sister's back doorstep the next day to drop off the clothes, he found Nate playing trucks on the kitchen floor, Ryan at the stove and Betsy nowhere to be seen.

Betsy, Ryan informed him, was out having lunch and shopping with friends. He was in charge of providing a nutritious meal for their son.

Though Keenan had doubts about Ryan's cooking abilities, he accepted his friend's invitation to stay for a "nutritious" lunch.

The orange slices Ryan tossed on each of their plates were hard to screw up, but the grilled cheese sandwich had gone beyond well-done to burnt. Keenan decided to start the meal with a good stiff shot of no-name cola.

Ryan lifted a glass of milk to his lips. He'd told Keenan he was drinking the white stuff because he wanted to set a good example for Nate. "How was the birthday party?"

"It wasn't a birthday party. It was a *quinceañera*." Keenan took another sip of the cola. "For the daughter of one of Mitzi's office employees."

"I wish Bets and I could afford to have someone come in and clean." Ryan glanced into the living room strewn with toys and blocks. "You're lucky."

"What are you talking about?" Keenan took a bit of sandwich, trying to ignore the blackened bread. "The boardinghouse doesn't employ a cleaning service."

Ryan took a bite of his sandwich, frowned. He flipped it over, sighed, and then began to scrape off the charred parts with a butter knife. He stopped for a second to glance at his son, who was eating the sandwich he'd cut up for him without complaint.

"C'mon, Keenan." Ryan dropped the sandwich to his plate. "Everyone knows you're practically living with rich—and incredibly hot—Dr. Sanchez."

The chunk of bread that had been sliding quite nicely down Keenan's throat came to an abrupt halt. It took a big gulp of soda to wash it the rest of the way down.

"I live at the boardinghouse." His tone dared Ryan to disagree. "Mitzi and I are friends."

Ryan cocked his head. "Friends with benefits?"

Keenan gave the charred sandwich in front of him one last look before pushing the plate to the side. He lifted his chin. "Friends."

Ryan gave a snort, worthy of any of the bulls he used to ride. He started to speak but was drowned out by his son.

HER KIND OF HERO | 157

"More," Nate bellowed. "Want more."

Most of the grilled cheese pieces remained on the high chair tray but the orange slices had disappeared.

"Say please," Ryan prompted when Nate banged his hand against the tray.

Nate's face took on a mulish expression.

"Say please," Ryan said again.

The little boy gave his father an angelic smile. "Pease."

"That's my boy." Ryan tousled his son's dark hair and dropped several orange pieces onto the tray.

"Go slow," Ryan warned, when the boy started shoveling them in. "And eat your sandwich, too."

"Puffy eat." Nate swept his arm across the tray and pieces of grilled cheese rained down on the Pomeranian waiting at his feet. "Yucky."

Keenan suppressed a smile when the child turned back to the orange slices. He had a feeling Ryan and Betsy were going to have their hands full with their little buckaroo.

Once the dog pranced off with the chunk of sandwich in her mouth, Ryan turned to Keenan. "You realize that Mitzi and I went out a couple of times. We were just friends, too."

A knot formed in the pit of Keenan's stomach. "Friends with benefits?"

Ryan laughed so uproariously that Nate shrieked and waved his arms excitedly.

"Heck, no," Ryan managed to sputter when he finally stopped laughing. "She wouldn't let me touch her. Not even a kiss. I decided she must be a cold fish."

"No," Keenan said, thinking of her warmth, her passion and the scorching heat that flared whenever they were together. "Not cold at all."

"What you're saying is I wasn't her type."

"That lawyer brain is firing on all circuits today."

"The doctor is hot for you."

"For now. Until she finds Mr. Right."

Obviously confused, Ryan cocked his head. "I thought *you* were Mr. Right."

"I'm a placeholder." Keenan's laugh held no humor as he thought of Mitzi's list. "Until the right guy appears."

"Does that bother you?"

Keenan started to deny it, and then reconsidered. If he could talk to anyone about his jumbled feelings, it'd be Ry.

"It didn't at first," he admitted. "Somewhere along the way, things changed. At least for me."

"You're in love with her."

The words hung there like a red flag, waving between them in the breeze.

"Yeah, I love her." Keenan scowled. "Now I have to decide what I'm going to do about it."

When Keenan headed for the Clippety Do-Dah Salon Thursday afternoon, he still hadn't decided what he was going to do about his feelings for Mitzi. He considered telling her he loved her. Then he wondered if that would just make things awkward and ruin what time he had left with her.

He'd never told a woman he loved her. Because Mitzi was the first woman he ever loved. He didn't want to be a placeholder. Heck, he didn't want to even be her boyfriend.

He wanted to marry her. He wanted to be her husband.

Husband.

The word pulled him up short.

Marriage. To Mitzi. Was it really such a crazy thought?

Yes, he told himself with increased agitation, it was crazy to even think of it, much less consider it an option.

Mitzi was a doctor, for chrissakes. Established. Ready to settle

HER KIND OF HERO | 159

down. She was building a million-dollar home in an exclusive subdivision of Jackson Hole.

While he didn't believe himself to be less than any other man, Keenan was also a realist. Mitzi was ready to settle down while he was starting over.

But if he loved her and she loved him...

He pulled his thoughts up short. That was really the crux of the matter. What did she feel for him?

If she did love him, why couldn't they build a life together? He was driven to succeed. He would work hard, be as successful in his chosen field as she was in hers. If she'd just give him a chance...

"Keenan."

He jerked his head up and realized he'd reached the salon.

Cassidy's smile was wide and friendly and the tension gripping his shoulders eased.

"Ready to go blue?" the hairstylist asked. "It's a delightfully delectable color and it's trending right now."

His gaze lingered on her short choppy hair, streaked royal blue and platinum. "Looks good on you."

"Aren't you a sweet man." Her smile widened with pleasure.

Looking at her now, at the wide smile on her face, his heart warmed. He recalled the child who'd worn a Halloween catsuit every day to kindergarten, a little girl from the wrong side of the tracks whom teachers labeled quirky. Even back then Keenan had known that survival took many forms.

Remembering—understanding—spawned a rush of brotherly affection. While he and Betsy had each other, Cassidy had been the sole sane one in that dysfunctional house at the end of the block.

"If you and Dr. Sanchez go Splitsville, you know where to find me," Cassidy said in a loud whisper.

Impulsively, Keenan looped a companionable arm around her

shoulder and planted a noisy kiss on her cheek. "Cassidy, darlin', you'll be the first one I call."

Like a missile, red shot up her cheeks. She cleared her throat then gestured with her head. "Your honey arrived early."

Keenan turned toward a row of chairs to find the doctor sitting patiently while one of Cassidy's associates wrapped little pieces of foil in her hair.

Her eyes met Keenan. She raised a brow.

Releasing Cassidy's arm, he strolled over to Mitzi. When he got close, he stopped, cocked his head. "I can't picture you as a blue-head."

"Would it insult you if I admitted I have no problem picturing you with blue spiky hair?"

He laughed. God, he loved this woman.

"You'll look elegant, as always." He heaved an exaggerated sigh. "While I will resemble a Blue Man Group castoff."

"If you'd like, you can sit right here, Keenan." Cassidy gestured to the chair next to Mitzi, casting the doctor an apologetic look. "That way the two of you can talk while you go blue."

"Great." Keenan plopped into the chair before Mitzi could respond.

Cassidy studied his hair with an experienced eye. "While you're here, should I trim it up?"

Keenan slanted a sideways glance at Mitzi. Though it was longer than he normally liked, she'd told him more than once how much she liked running her fingers through it when they made love.

But her face was expressionless, telling him nothing.

"Not today," he said. "If I change my mind, I'll come back."

Cassidy raked her fingers through the dark strands. "You have nice hair. Thick and silky."

Mitzi's lips curved in the slightest of smiles. This time when his gaze met hers, it held and he felt the connection.

Getting his hair colored didn't take as long as Keenan had

HER KIND OF HERO | 161

anticipated. Cassidy talked nonstop to both him and Mitzi, while her associate, a waif named Daffodil Prentiss, focused on Mitzi's hair.

When they finished, the doctor's hair was dark with a ribbon of deep blue running through the auburn strands. Cassidy had taken a different approach with his and colored only the tips.

The good news was one haircut and the color would be gone. The bad news was the tips were an eye-popping electric blue.

Had he really expected subtlety from Cassidy Kaye?

"Do you like it?" she asked Mitzi, looking surprisingly anxious.

"Why are you asking her?" Keenan asked. "It's my hair."

"She's the one who has to look at it," Cassidy shot back.

To his surprise, Mitzi stepped closer and slid her fingers through his hair in a possessive gesture. Keenan wasn't into female messages, but to him, it clearly said, he's mine.

"I like it," Mitzi declared. "Sexy."

Without warning, the heat, the electricity, the intense emotion that filled the air whenever they were close, scorched his blood.

"Hoo-kay, then." Cassidy smiled brightly. "Thank you both for coming in."

Mitzi opened her purse.

Keenan reached for his wallet.

Before they could pull out a credit card or a single bill, Cassidy shook her head firmly. "Doing everyone's hair is my donation. If you want to give more, add it to the fund."

Mitzi dropped the wallet back into her purse. "Thank you, Cassidy." Her gaze shifted to the blonde. "You, too, Daffy."

The girl with the large violet eyes and straight wheat-colored hair smiled shyly. "The color is temporary but it should last about two weeks. It's a good look for you. If you decide to keep it, stop back. I'll retouch it."

"That goes for you, too, Mr. McGregor." Cassidy's booming

voice stood in stark contrast to Daffy's whisper-soft words. "I imagine in a couple of weeks, you'll be ready to get those ends trimmed."

Keenan resisted glancing at Mitzi. "Thanks, Cass."

"Thank me by getting more donations," Cassidy told him. "Now, you two get out of here so Daffy and I can clean up and get the heck out of Dodge."

They were on the sidewalk and turning the corner when Keenan took Mitzi's arm. "That hair of yours is a real turn-on."

She laughed. "Everything is a turn-on for you."

"Everything about you, anyway," he admitted. "Let's head to your place and get out of these clothes."

"That's subtle."

"I don't feel subtle right now." He slid his palm down her arm. "I wanted you naked a half hour ago."

"Was that before or after you laid that kiss on Cassidy?" Though her tone was light, there was an edge to her voice that hadn't been there seconds earlier.

Keenan realized he owed her an explanation. If he'd seen her kiss some other guy, no matter how casual, he'd want an explanation. Heck, he'd demand one. "Cass and I, we go way back."

Surprise skittered across Mitzi's face.

"We were neighbors," he continued. "I felt like a big brother. But I wasn't always able to protect her, not like I could Bets."

All sorts of questions sprang to mind, but Mitzi swallowed them. Sadness had filled Keenan's eyes and she sensed that any further talk on the subject would kill any possibility of her getting him naked that evening.

He wasn't the only one who wanted that, she realized.

She'd watched him saunter into Clippety Do-Dah and had studied him as if he were a stranger. Tall, broad-shouldered with hair the color of mahogany, he cut an imposing figure in work jeans, boots and a faded T-shirt.

There was a confidence, a strength to him that was compelling.

Irritation had surged when she'd watched Cassidy flirt with him. When he'd leaned over and kissed her, Mitzi felt as if someone had taken a scalpel to her heart.

Mine, she'd almost called out with a possessive fury that surprised her with its intensity. *Get your hands off my man.*

Instead, she'd restrained her temper and silently fumed. It was silly, she knew. They were only friends. The trouble was what had blossomed between them no longer felt like simple friendship.

"Let's go home." Impulsively she took his hand and experienced a rush of pleasure when his fingers laced through hers. "I want to be with you. Just you. Just me."

CHAPTER SEVENTEEN

There was only one thing Mitzi was hungry for when they got to her house...and it wasn't in the refrigerator. It was found in the man standing before her, his arms now wrapped around her waist.

The second they'd walked through the front door, she'd been ready to strip and jump him. Before that could happen, he'd pulled her into his arms and simply held her close.

"I love—" he stopped to nuzzle the sensitive skin behind her ear "—your hair."

"Wish I could say the same thing about yours." Mitzi leaned her head back, reveling in his touch.

"It's bold, that's for sure." He softly laughed. "I'm not sure anyone but Cass could pull off electric blue."

Mitzi slid her fingers through his hair. "I'm glad you didn't cut it."

"Feeling your fingers combing through it is one of my favorite pleasures." His hazel eyes remained focused on her. "Spending time with you is another."

She fought the urge to tell him it was the same for her, that

HER KIND OF HERO | 165

seeing him was the best part of her day. How would he respond if she told him she was falling in love with him?

Mitzi wasn't sure why the thought scared her so much, but it did. Enough that she had to put an end to the conversation.

"I want you, Keenan."

His eyes never left her. "I feel the same about you."

Once again uneasiness swept over her like a harsh November wind. "In bed."

A flicker of his eyelashes was his only response.

She linked her fingers with his and stepped from his arms. "Now."

"I won't disappoint you, Mitzi," he said abruptly, his expression intense, almost fierce.

"You never have." She offered a reassuring smile. "You and me, we're the dynamic duo."

"Dynamic duo, eh?" His lips twitched. "Okay, tonight I'll be Superman. You can be Lois Lane."

"No way." Mitzi felt some of the tightness around her heart ease at the lighthearted teasing. "I'm Wonder Woman."

"Diana and Bruce?" Keenan thought for a second, flashed a smile. "Batman does have a cool car."

"A car doesn't figure in my fantasies tonight."

"No backseat for you? Not even if it was the Batmobile?"

Her heart stuttered. "I might make an exception for the Batmobile. But tonight I prefer a nice soft bed."

"You're such a traditionalist," he teased.

She stepped close and planted a bite on his shoulder hard enough to make him yelp. "Let's see if you feel that same way after I get through with you."

"The way I feel will never change," he murmured as his lips closed over hers.

～

The next morning Mitzi found herself more confused than ever. She'd deliberately set out to make their lovemaking erotic and mind-numbing, trying to avoid any emotion.

His playful humor, his willingness to embrace whatever game she wanted to play, only endeared him more to her. She had to admit that no matter how hot it got between them, there was something in his touch, in his taste, in the explosion that rocked her world that said this was someone who mattered, someone she could fully trust.

That was the part that frightened her most, she realized as she lay in bed, listening to the shower run. He'd slipped from the bed at six, cognizant of the fact his coworkers would be arriving within the hour to put the final finishing touches on the home.

Because she didn't know what he'd see in her eyes, she kept hers closed and pretended to sleep. She didn't have any surgeries this morning and her first patient wasn't scheduled until ten o'clock, so there was no reason to jump right up.

Still keeping her eyes shut, Mitzi heard Keenan come out of the bathroom and rummage in the bottom dresser drawer where he kept some clothes.

Mitzi opened her eyes to tiny slits, just wide enough to see him standing at the dresser, his back to her. He had a fine body and a very excellent backside.

She'd dated handsome, athletic men before, had even slept with some of them. She realized that she'd never opened her heart to them, never let them get truly close.

Until she met Keenan, she'd never found anyone she trusted enough to let inside her head. Inside her heart. Only her friend Kate knew her better than Keenan did now.

The question was—where did they go from here? Because she had no answer, she made sure her eyes were closed and her breathing regular when he turned to her.

He stood over the bed for a long moment, then leaned over

and brushed a light kiss across her forehead. "Later, Wonder Woman."

"I love you, Batman," she whispered softly as the door clicked closed behind him. "And, despite my superpowers, I'm not sure I'm brave enough to do anything about it."

As the end of the weekend neared, Mitzi still hadn't come to a decision on how to deal with her growing feelings—okay, her *love*—for Keenan. When she'd made it clear she was looking for a husband, he'd been equally clear that his goal was to get his footing and start to take back his life. He'd even admitted he wasn't ready for a serious relationship.

Although Mitzi wasn't a worrier, she was concerned how a confession of love might change things between them...especially after she'd continually insisted they were just friends. And he hadn't argued. Not once.

Until Keenan, no man had touched her heart. She loved him and the life they'd started to forge together. She, who was easily bored with the predictable, treasured the routines they'd established.

Routines like "movie night." She and Keenan had fallen into the Sunday evening habit of going out for pizza then coming home and watching a movie. They'd mark the end of the weekend by cuddling on the sofa with a bowl of popcorn and tall glasses of soda in front of the screen.

She'd been excited about the comedy they'd picked for tonight. Then, Steve had called. Though Mitzi could tell Keenan was excited about the flight that would take him all the way to the eastern edge of Nebraska, her heart had sunk.

Not only would Keenan be gone the rest of the day, but he wouldn't be back until tomorrow. No afternoon hike around Jenny Lake as planned. No pizza and movie this evening. No warm body snuggled against hers when she awoke in the morning. No Keenan.

When she dropped him off at the boardinghouse so he could pick up his car to go to the airport, she'd surprised them both by wrapping her arms around his neck and holding him tight for several heartbeats.

"Stay safe," was all she'd said. All she could manage to say.

As Mitzi drove away, she knew the dark cloud now hanging over her had nothing to do with the weather. Once home, it didn't help her mood when she tripped running to answer the phone. She fell, rapping her head smartly against the edge of the rustic coffee table. Knowing it could be the hospital calling, Mitzi pulled to her feet and reached it before it went to voice mail. "This is Mitzi Sanchez."

"*M'ija*, it's Mama."

Mitzi closed her eyes for a moment. She took a deep breath, let it out slowly and spoke in Spanish. "How are you?"

While her mother updated her on her sister, her nieces and the ladies at the church, Mitzi took a gel pack from the freezer and pressed it against her throbbing head. She was washing down ibuprofen with a cola when her mother mentioned the increased difficulty she was having getting around.

The complaints weren't anything new. Back when Mitzi was still in medical school, her mother's doctor had sent her to an orthopedic surgeon. The specialist had recommended a total knee replacement. Her mother had refused. How could she watch her grandchildren if she had surgery?

"I've got a solution to your problem, Mama." Mitzi stroked the cat that had jumped onto her lap. "One of my associates, Dr. Benedict Campbell, is a knee specialist. You could have the surgery here then stay and recover at my home."

She listened to her mother detail all the reasons why coming to Jackson Hole wasn't a good idea.

"Yes, I do work a lot of hours." Mitzi did her best to keep her

HER KIND OF HERO | 169

tone even. "I have a housekeeper who could be here when I was gone. She could—"

When her mother interrupted with more excuses and mentioned Mitzi's sister thought she simply needed another injection, Mitzi gave up. She tried to massage away a burgeoning headache, and then winced when her fingers touched the bump on her forehead.

The conversation was drawing to a close—or so Mitzi hoped—when her mother asked if anything was new. Mitzi thought about mentioning the award she'd be receiving but decided why bother.

In her mother's eyes, nothing she did was ever good enough or worthy of a word of praise. That had been true when she was a child, and it was true now. And despite Mitzi's successful career and her sister's continued screwups, her mother would continue to go to her eldest daughter for advice, rather than her.

Knowing that didn't hurt much anymore. Only sometimes. Like now.

Mitzi said goodbye, determined not to give in to self-pity. She'd eat. Watch a movie. Go to bed.

She opened the freezer door and scanned the contents. She wrinkled her nose and shut the door. She didn't want a frozen chicken breast. She wanted pizza.

Before Keenan had come into the picture, she'd eaten alone plenty of times. There was no reason she couldn't have dinner at Perfect Pizza then come back and enjoy the movie.

Just because Keenan wasn't there didn't mean she couldn't have a nice evening. Even as Mitzi changed clothes and headed out the door, she couldn't deny that being part of a dynamic duo trumped being a lonely single any day of the week.

It was still early when Mitzi reached the doors of the popular pizza parlor in downtown Jackson. She figured the dinner rush wouldn't hit for another hour. Before placing her order at the counter, she considered getting the pie to go but decided to enjoy a couple of slices in the restaurant first.

Once she ordered, Mitzi got her drink and took her salad to a table by the window. Pulling out the latest *AAOS Journal,* she settled in to read about the "Management of Nonunion Following Surgical Management of Scaphoid Fractures" while she waited for her pizza.

"I didn't expect to see you here."

Mitzi glanced up from the journal and saw Betsy. Looking Sunday-night casual in jeans and a sage-colored hoodie, Keenan's sister's smile was friendly, even as her gaze darted around the dining area.

Betsy cocked her head. "Where's Keenan?"

As Betsy and Ryan hadn't been at the café this morning when Keenan took the call, it was an understandable question.

"He flew to Omaha this afternoon. He won't be back until tomorrow."

"Oh," Betsy said.

This time it was Mitzi who glanced around the dining area. "Are Ryan and the baby with you?"

"They're home. Nate fell asleep and I was in the mood to get out of the house, so I volunteered to pick up a pizza."

"I'm waiting for one, too." Mitzi gestured to a chair. "Join me. We can kill time together."

As soon as Betsy took a seat in the chair opposite her, Mitzi realized this was the chance she'd been waiting for, an opportunity to set things right between them. Mitzi opened her mouth, but Betsy spoke first.

"It must seem strange not to have Keenan around." Betsy flushed when Mitzi cocked her head. "I mean, lately you two have been inseparable. Last week we invited him over for Sunday-night dinner, but he told us that's your 'movie night.'"

Mitzi gave a little laugh. "We've become like a couple of old

HER KIND OF HERO | 171

people holding to our routines, but he certainly should have accepted your invitation."

"Ryan and I love our little routines, too."

Mitzi exchanged a smile of understanding with Betsy. As much as she was enjoying the conversation, she needed to get some business out of the way first.

"Your brother is a wonderful man." Mitzi held Betsy's gaze. "I'm so incredibly sorry about what I said that night. I was wrong. Totally, completely, wrong. And I hope you will forgive me."

There was no reason to go into detail on what night she was referring to or what was said; they both remembered. Those stupid, thoughtless words she'd uttered had become the elephant in the room whenever their paths crossed.

"It sounds like you care about Keenan," Betsy said slowly, as if having difficulty wrapping her mind around the notion. "Genuinely care."

Mitzi cleared her throat, took a sip of her iced tea. "I do."

"I'm glad to hear it." Betsy's eyes darkened with worry. "How is he doing today?"

Mitzi straightened and concern wrapped tightly around her like a too-small sweater. "He's fine. Why wouldn't he be fine?"

Betsy shifted her gaze out the window for several seconds. "Today is, was," she corrected, "our mother's birthday."

"Gloria's birthday?"

Surprise flickered in Betsy's eyes. "He's spoken of her?"

"Keenan has nothing good to say about her."

"She was horrible to him."

"Why?" Mitzi's confusion was real. Who could be mean to a nice guy like Keenan?

"Crazy as it sounds, I think it was because he has such a good heart. Though, after the incident with the flowers, he rarely let that side of him show, except to me."

Though Mitzi hadn't yet heard the story, anger at the faceless Gloria had begun to build.

"What happened?" A cold chill settled over Mitzi. "What did she do to him?"

"Our mother was a Jekyll and Hyde. Probably because of the drinking. Or maybe that's what led her to drink. I don't know, but right before her birthday that year Mom seemed better. We'd even done a few fun things as a family. I was five. Keenan was ten." Betsy closed her eyes for a second. "For her birthday he gave her flowers he'd picked from the neighbor's yard."

Betsy's eyes grew bleak. Tears welled up but didn't fall.

Mitzi knew the story was about to take a bad turn and her heart wrenched for the man she loved.

Snatching a couple of napkins from the table dispenser, Mitzi pressed one into Betsy's hand and kept the other for herself.

Betsy dabbed at her eyes and cleared her throat. "Keenan didn't know Gloria had started drinking that morning right after he left for school. She was a mean drunk."

Mitzi balled her hands into fists, and when she spoke her voice was ice. "Tell me what she did."

Betsy met Mitzi's gaze. "She flung the flowers in his face and said she didn't want a bunch of stupid weeds. I still remember the shock in his eyes. He didn't cry, not really."

Mitzi could scarcely breathe past the tightness gripping her chest.

"The pain he tried so hard to hide fueled her anger." Betsy's eyes darkened with memories as she continued. "She pushed him around, taunting, telling him he needed to toughen up. Told him if he put his heart out there, he'd better be prepared to have someone stomp it, because that's what always happened."

"He was a little boy. Just a child," Mitzi murmured.

"Not after that day." Betsy's voice broke.

"Your mother was a monster." Mitzi spat the words, tears leaking from her eyes, but she didn't care.

Betsy's gaze searched Mitzi's face. A ghost of a smile touched her lips. "You love my brother."

HER KIND OF HERO | 173

"Who doesn't love Keenan?"

"Before you, he'd never trusted a woman. So hear me on this, Mitzi." Steel filled Betsy's voice. "If you hurt my brother, you'll answer to me."

Odd, but the fierceness on Betsy's face comforted Mitzi. She liked knowing Keenan had a strong ally in his sister.

"He's lucky to have you and Ryan in his corner."

"A fact we remind him of all the time."

As she'd probably intended, Betsy's quip lightened the mood.

Mitzi thought of the former bull-riding-champion-turned-attorney. She remembered the stricken look on Betsy's face the time Mitzi had strode into a party with the man Betsy secretly loved at her side. Yes, she still had some making up to do.

"Other than friendship, there was never anything between me and your husband," Mitzi blurted out.

Betsy waved a dismissive hand. "That was a long time ago, way before Ryan and I got together."

"I never slept with him," Mitzi assured her. "We didn't even kiss."

She'd never thought of Ryan as anything more than a friend. Not like Keenan. With him, friendship had never been enough.

"Ryan told me," Betsy said softly. "I appreciate you wanting to make it clear."

"I'd like it if you and I could be friends."

"I'd like that, too." Betsy reached across the table and squeezed Mitzi's hand. "In fact, I predict we'll end up being great friends. Which is fortunate, considering my brother is in love with you."

Mitzi's heart leaped even as she shifted uncomfortably in her seat. "Keenan has never, ah, said he loves me."

He'd shown it in so many ways. But he hadn't said the words to her. Not yet, anyway.

"I know my brother. What he feels is in his eyes every time he looks at you." Betsy's lips curved in satisfaction. "I see love in your eyes, as well. I'm happy for it. But please don't hurt him."

"I would never hurt him." Mitzi opened her mouth then shut it. If her goal was to protect her pride, this would be the time to lie and tell Betsy she wasn't sure what she felt for Keenan. Even though Mitzi knew without a doubt she was completely and irrevocably in love with him.

It was time to seize the moment, lay the cards on the table, face up.

Mitzi had been honest with herself.

Tonight, she'd be honest with Betsy.

Then it was time to be honest with Keenan.

CHAPTER EIGHTEEN

Mitzi had barely gotten home from Perfect Pizza when her phone rang. She smiled at the readout. "I miss you."

For a second silence was all she heard. Then Keenan chuckled. "Do you even know who this is?"

"Batman, of course." She lowered her voice to a seductive whisper. "Or should I call you Bruce?"

He laughed. "For now, why don't you call me Keenan? And hey, I miss you, too."

Mitzi smiled into the phone and dropped onto the sofa. Her mood, which had been partly cloudy only moments before, was now bright and sunny. "How's it going in Oma-ha?"

He told her about the flight and the small motel room where he was staying. As they talked about their days, she found comfort in sharing the mundane.

"I had a sub and chips for dinner," Keenan said. "I hated missing movie night."

"Bitty did her best to keep me company." Mitzi slanted a glance at the kitten, currently busy washing herself. "It wasn't the same. She didn't laugh once, and it was a really funny movie."

"Give her time. She's just a kitten. Her sense of humor is still developing."

"By the way..." Mitzi forced a lighthearted tone. "I ran into your sister when I was picking up the pizza."

"Betsy?"

"You have more than one sister?"

"Not as far as I know," he said easily. "Were she and Ryan having a date night?"

"Actually it was just her. She was picking up a pizza at the same time, so while we waited we sat and talked for a few minutes. We had a nice chat."

"What did you talk about?" he asked, and she heard the caution in his voice.

"Girl stuff mostly." Mitzi kept her tone light. "A little about men."

"Men?" His tone turned wary.

"I'll just say we bonded over our mutual admiration of the same man."

"Well," he said after a long moment, "you and Ryan had a history and —"

"Ryan," she sputtered. "We weren't talking about Ry—"

His laughter stopped her cold.

Mitzi shook her head and chuckled. "A couple of states away and you can still put one over on me."

"You and Betsy haven't had much to do with each other before."

There was a question in his voice. And she had the answer that would put his mind at ease.

"We'd gotten off on the wrong foot, which was totally my fault," she admitted. "We're okay now. In fact I'd say Betsy and I are on the road to becoming good friends."

There were a couple of seconds of silence before Keenan spoke, his voice husky. "Glad to hear it."

She heard the emotion in his words and realized their relationship—or lack of one—had troubled him more than he'd let on. Mitzi liked knowing she'd done something that made him happy and something that made her happy, as well.

As they continued to chat, Mitzi thought about bringing up Gloria but decided why put a downer on his evening. Better to end the call with a little phone sex.

After all, she'd discovered it was so much fun to get down and dirty with the one you loved. And, since Keenan hadn't mentioned Gloria, he'd probably forgotten it was his mother's birthday, anyway.

Keenan lay in the dark motel room and stared at the ceiling, his mind too restless for sleep.

When Mitzi had told him she and Betsy had mended their fences, it was as if a heavy stone that had been weighing him down had been cast aside. Until that moment Keenan hadn't realized how much it mattered that the two women he loved most in the world liked each other.

Now, it was time to forge ahead, to take the next step.

He knew Mitzi cared. He felt it in her touch. He saw it when she looked at him and her eyes turned soft. But did she love him? Ah, that was the million-dollar question. He thought she did, hoped she did. Because he loved her.

Truly. Madly. Deeply.

Such intense emotion made him feel like a first-rate sap.

Keenan knew, given the chance, he could make Mitzi happy. He believed he understood her better than anyone else. Just as she understood him.

He hoped she loved him, as well.

"You're a fool if you think she wants you." In the utter stillness, he heard his mother's voice, dripping with scorn and derision. *"You're nothing. A nobody. A mutt without a pot to pee in."*

How many times had Gloria said those same words to him when he'd asked a girl on a date? How many times had she flashed that I-told-you-so smirk when one had refused or dumped him?

You didn't even make the top ten of Mitzi's husband list. What makes you suddenly number one?

This time it was *his* voice sowing the seeds of doubt.

Keenan screwed his lids shut. He would not give in to fear. During his three years in prison, he'd learned to fight for what he wanted and to persevere. Though the journey back to freedom had been difficult and filled with setbacks, he hadn't given up.

He wouldn't give up now.

He would let Mitzi know what was in his heart.

Where they went from here...would be up to her.

It was early afternoon when Keenan landed in Jackson. Though he wanted to see Mitzi, he knew she'd be tied up with patients for at least three more hours. The positive side was it gave him the opportunity to take care of some overdue business. He raked a hand through his hair.

It was time for the electric blue to go.

Keenan leaned comfortably against the wing of the plane that had safely taken him from Wyoming to Nebraska and back, enjoying the feel of the sun against his face. By mid-October there was often snow in Jackson. So far this year the fall had been unseasonably mild.

Slipping the phone from his jacket pocket, he was scrolling through his contact list when the phone rang.

After thanking him for making the trip to Nebraska, Steve asked him to stop by the office before he headed for home.

Home. Was it wrong that the word conjured up an image of Mitzi's house? Of the kitchen with its striking contrasts of rough

HER KIND OF HERO | 179

and rugged with smooth and polished. Of a great room with rustic beams and glossy wood floor, most of which he'd laid himself. Of a small gray kitten in the arms of a woman who could make his heart melt with just one smile.

Keenan made his way across the airfield and found Steve standing outside the low-slung building that housed his office, enjoying a cola and the sunshine. "What's up, boss man?"

"Good news." Steve's normally booming voice sounded extra hearty. "Loretta Van Ness, one of our best clients, is stopping by to discuss increasing the services we provide to her company. If she follows through—and it sounds like a done deal to me—I'd like to assign you to the account."

For a second, Keenan could only stare. "Would this be—"

"Part-time at first. You'd have regular hours and some benefits. I can see it increasing to full-time in the future. Or, we could add another account and get you close to full-time. Interested?"

Try as he might, Keenan couldn't stop the dopey grin. "Very."

"I'll let you know—" Steve's gaze shifted to behind Keenan, and his smile widened in welcome. "Mrs. Van Ness, we were just talking about you."

Turning, Keenan studied the mid-sixties woman with pewter gray hair styled short, an aristocratic face and cool blue eyes. Her navy suit and matching shoes probably cost more than he made in six months.

She tilted her head. "I'm not sure I like being the subject of idle conversation."

The lilt in her voice took the edge from the words.

"Keenan here is one of our best pilots." Steve jerked a thumb in his direction. "I was speaking with him about taking over your account. He'll do right by you."

"Keenan?"

"Yes, ma'am." Resisting the urge to wipe suddenly sweaty palms against his jeans, he extended his hand. "Keenan McGregor. I'm pleased to meet you."

The woman's lily-white hand dropped like a stone to her side even as her gaze flicked over him dismissively, lingering for perhaps an extra beat on his hair. She sniffed as if she smelled something foul.

Steve froze for a few seconds then began to babble. "Keenan is very involved in the community. He raised almost a thousand dollars by collecting pledges and agreeing to dye his hair blue. It's part of the Go Blue for a Cure, to raise—"

"I'm well aware of that particular fund-raiser," Mrs. Van Ness interrupted, speaking directly to Steve and ignoring Keenan completely. "What you're apparently not aware of is this man's mother ran my grandson off the road while he was riding his bike, causing extensive facial trauma. It's a miracle Anthony wasn't killed."

Keenan hadn't been in Jackson when a drunken Gloria had smashed her car into a tree, killing herself. He'd heard she'd been driving erratically and narrowly missed hitting a kid on a bike. Until this moment he hadn't realized the boy had been injured.

"I will not have anyone associated with that horrid woman fly my cargo or my employees anywhere." Though the woman's hands grasped her purse so tightly her knuckles were white, her face remained cool and composed. "As my deceased husband always used to say, the apple never falls far from the tree."

A frigid cold swept through Keenan, the chill going straight to the bone. He remained where he stood, stiff as any soldier, the pleasant smile he'd flashed earlier frozen on his lips.

"Mrs. Van Ness," Steve protested. "It hardly seems fair to hold—"

"Let me remind you that there are other charter services in Jackson Hole, Mr. Kowalski." The woman bit out the words in an imperious tone. "The fact that you even employ this man makes me doubt your good sense. In fact, I may pull all my business. I'll let you know my decision in that regard tomorrow."

Turning on her heel, Mrs. Van Ness returned to her shiny pearl-white Escalade and drove off without a backward glance.

Keenan stood silent beside Steve as they watched the taillights disappear from view.

There was apology in Steve's eyes when he turned to Keenan. "I realize I said the job was yours but—"

"No worries," Keenan spoke quickly, his voice gruff. He cleared his throat and tried again. "The client is within her rights to refuse a pilot."

"She'll come around."

They both knew that was a lie. Mrs. Van Ness wasn't going to change her mind. Keenan wasn't even sure he blamed her. Gloria had hurt her grandchild.

The only question remaining was, if she pushed to get him off the Grand Teton payroll, would Steve succumb to her threats?

Because Steve Kowalski was a businessman first, Keenan had a feeling he already knew what the answer to that question would be.

Mitzi resisted the urge to pull out her phone and check for messages. Instead she smiled brightly at Dr. Noah Anson, Jackson Hole's new neurosurgeon.

Several hours earlier she'd received a brief text from Keenan telling her he'd landed safely and he'd give her a call later. Mitzi hadn't heard from him since. She'd called him but it had gone straight to voice mail.

She'd left a detailed message telling him Dr. John Campbell had insisted all the doctors in the practice attend the Jackson Young Professionals meeting this evening. Ben's father wanted to make sure Dr. Anson was properly welcomed to the community. Mitzi asked Keenan to meet her at the brewery where the event was being held.

So far, he'd been a no-show.

Mitzi shoved aside her worry and focused on the man at her side. Tall and lean with hair so dark it might have been black and brilliant blue eyes, Noah wore his hand-tailored suit with the casual elegance of those born to wealth.

Though he seemed nice enough, Mitzi swore she saw a flash of disapproval in his eyes when he'd noticed the strands of blue in her hair. And, in trying to figure out whom they might know in common, Noah had dropped a significant amount of prominent names.

Mitzi wished Keenan was here. Afterward, they could laugh about the man's pompousness, critique the food, then forget it all and make love.

But he wasn't here. Temper fought with worry.

Where the heck was he?

Wouldn't she have heard if there'd been a car crash? Mitzi tightened her fingers around the stem of her wineglass. On her way over here from the clinic, she'd tried to reach him a fifth—or was it sixth?—time. Once again her call had gone straight to voice mail. Other than the brief text, she'd heard nothing.

"Jackson Hole seems like a beautiful place. It'd be nice if I had someone to show me around."

Mitzi blinked and realized that in a roundabout way the new doctor was asking her to play tour guide. How would she get out of this one?

"I'm sure Dr. Sanchez would be happy to show you around," Dr. John Campbell, Ben's father and the head of Spring Gulch Orthopedics, said smoothly.

The man terrified her. Even when she and Ben had been dating, she'd never gotten good vibes from his father. According to Poppy, now Ben's wife, "John" was a sweet man, a wonderful father-in-law and a loving grandfather. *Sweet* wasn't a side of the steely-eyed doctor that Mitzi had ever seen.

She knew Dr. Campbell wanted Noah to be happy in Jackson

HER KIND OF HERO | 183

Hole. Many of the procedures that could have been done in town had there been a neurosurgeon available as a cosurgeon had been forced to go elsewhere. Now they could retain the business in Jackson Hole and make it easier on patients. A win-win for everyone.

"I'd be happy to show you around." Mitzi offered him her brightest smile as Dr. Campbell slipped away, leaving the two of them alone again.

Before she could say another word, her phone rang. She recognized the ringtone she assigned to her "favorite" contacts. Mitzi offered an apologetic smile. "I'm sorry. I need to take this."

"Understood."

Mitzi stepped away, relief flooding her. But when she glanced at the readout, she realized it was Kate calling, not Keenan. "Hey, Ms. No-Show. I thought you were going to be at this shindig. Instead, I'm here all alone. Excluding, of course, the dozens of other people who did show up."

"I planned to come," Kate assured her. "At the last second some of the Stone Craft employees decided to celebrate Joel's birthday at Wally's Place tonight."

The popular bar in downtown Jackson had peanuts on every table, a mechanical bull and five-dollar pitchers of beer. Every so often Mitzi had been known to ride the bull and do a little singing on the karaoke stage.

"I thought Joel's birthday was Saturday."

"It is, but tonight is Burger Night at Wally's, so the guys decided to celebrate early. It works out best since Joel and I are taking the kids to Yellowstone for the weekend."

Mitzi fought the dark cloud forming overhead. First Keenan went MIA. Now her best friend had bailed on her.

"Actually it's been a lot of fun so far." Kate raised her voice to be heard over the music and laughter. "Why don't you pop over once you're done there?"

"I don't know. It's been a long day—"

184 | CINDY KIRK

"Don't give me that. Besides, Keenan is here. Don't you want to see him?"

"Keenan?"

"Yeah, he got back from Nebraska this afternoon." Kate's voice became muffled. "I'd love to play darts. Mitz, I've got a dart game calling my name. Come over. Join us."

Kate ended the call. Mitzi stood staring at the phone.

Noah sidled up to her. "Everything okay?"

The concern in his voice sounded surprisingly genuine.

"I'm not sure," Mitzi said. "I'm just not sure."

CHAPTER NINETEEN

Though Wally's Place held a larger-than-normal crowd for a Monday night, Keenan sat alone at the end of the bar until Bill strolled over and confiscated the adjacent stool. His friend now sat silently nursing a beer and munching on peanuts.

"Did you ever want something so bad it made you feel weak?" Keenan injected a casual tone to his voice at odds with the tension gripping his chest.

If Bill thought the question strange, it didn't show. He merely lifted his glass, nodded as he surveyed the amber liquid. "I've been there a time or two."

That was all he said. Keenan told himself he was relieved Bill didn't ask any questions. The last thing he wanted to talk about was his troubles with Mitzi. He wasn't sure why he'd even made the comment.

After taking a sip of club soda, Keenan gazed around the cowboy bar. It had everything you'd expect: plank floors strewn with peanut shells, pool tables, dartboards and even a mechanical bull.

Though his mother had preferred the dives farther downtown for her drinking, simply being in a bar brought back memories of all the times she'd dragged him along with her. He'd sit in a dark corner and watch her get louder and meaner with each drink.

"Joel seems to be enjoying the evening," Bill commented.

Keenan turned his head, saw his boss talking with a couple of his construction foremen, his arm looped around his wife's waist.

Keenan had seen the look of surprise in Kate's eyes when he'd walked through the door. As Mitzi's BFF, no doubt she knew that Mitzi was at the Young Professionals get-together and had assumed he'd be with her.

The truth was, Keenan hadn't wanted to face Mitzi. Had he really thought she could love him, would want to be his wife? Mitzi was smart, successful and the most beautiful woman in Jackson Hole. She deserved better than a mutt.

If Mrs. Van Ness had her way, he'd never get another job flying in Jackson Hole. If that happened he'd never achieve his goal of flying full-time. Never have his own plane. Forget starting a charter service one day. At least not in this town.

Building a successful career in Jackson Hole with Mitzi by his side had been a pipe dream, spun by a guy who ought to know better.

"Sometimes you have to let go of dreams," Keenan murmured.

"What's bothering you, son?" Bill's tone might be matter-of-fact, but a fatherly concern underscored the words.

Keenan shrugged.

"Tell me." Bill spoke quietly, a give-me-no-bull look on his face.

Deciding he might feel better if he got the incident at the airfield off his chest, Keenan relayed the facts.

Bill took a long drink of his beer and cracked open another peanut shell.

"Loretta isn't usually so unreasonable." Bill's expression turned pensive. "Tony's accident shook her hard."

"*Loretta?* You know the woman?" Keenan wasn't sure why he was surprised. Jackson Hole was a cohesive community.

HER KIND OF HERO | 187

"Went to school with her youngest brother." Bill grabbed more peanuts, jiggled them in his hand. "Though she was quite a bit older than Roger, over the years I've had more than a passing acquaintance with her."

"Well, the way it looks now, *Loretta* is going to get me canned."

"If that happens, it'll be a bad break," Bill said quietly. "Something deeper is eating at you."

"You're fishing in a dry pond, buddy."

"Let's talk for a minute about your doctor friend," Bill continued as if Keenan hadn't spoken. "Where is Dr. Mitzi this fine evening?"

"The Young Professionals group is meeting tonight."

"Why aren't you with her?"

Anger bubbled up inside Keenan, but he kept his voice cool. "Because I'm here."

"You asked if I'd ever wanted something so badly it made me weak." Bill cracked another shell, popped a peanut into his mouth, chewed thoughtfully. "It appears you want Mitzi but for some reason think you can't have her."

"She's a doctor, Bill," Keenan snapped. "I'm nothing."

A work-hardened hand clamped hard on his biceps. "Don't ever let me hear something so goddamn foolish come from your mouth again. You have everything to offer that young woman. Everything that matters, anyway. If you're too scared to take a chance, that's on you. If you tell her how you feel and she kicks you to the curb, she's not the one for you."

There was fierceness in Bill's eyes that Keenan hadn't seen before and a protectiveness that was again almost...fatherly. For a second, Keenan wondered what it would be like to have a dad, but he shook the thought away. What did he know of fathers? His had split before Betsy was born.

"Kicks me to the curb, eh?" Keenan gave a little laugh. "That's a great visual. Real encouraging."

"You've got the mettle to go after your dreams, Keenan. Give

Mitzi a chance to show she's the kind of woman who sticks by her man even when he's down." Bill took a gulp of beer. "Pick up some flowers on your way. There's not a woman alive who doesn't love flowers."

Mitzi briefly considered stopping at Wally's Place on her way home from the brewery but at the last second turned her car toward the highway. She refused to run after Keenan.

I'm not his keeper. I'm not his wife. I'm not even important enough for him to call back.

The last hurt the most. Mutual respect and consideration had always been at the base of what they shared. That's why having Keenan ignore her calls didn't make any sense.

Had there been any indication of unhappiness last night when they'd talked? Anything she might have missed?

Recalling the call in vivid detail, her lips curved. No, all indications were they'd both been well pleased when they finally whispered good-night.

By the time she reached home, Mitzi's insides were twisty-tied in knots. Too wound up to sit, she flung her purse on the sofa and prowled the room. Bitty watched from atop the sofa, green eyes tracking her every move.

Mitzi didn't like feeling so out of control, didn't like it one bit. The next time she saw Keenan she'd blast him, let him know she wouldn't tolerate being treated with such disrespect.

"I am so angry at him, Bitty," Mitzi told the kitten. "If he showed up now, I might just slam the door in his face."

The doorbell rang and as Mitzi crossed to answer, Bitty regarded her thoughtfully through emerald-green eyes.

HER KIND OF HERO | 189

Keenan held the bouquet of flowers in a death grip. He didn't know why he'd picked them up. Flowers weren't his thing. He didn't give women flowers, not since he was ten years old. He told himself this was different. Mitzi was different.

When he left Just Blooms, he had every intention of confessing his love and asking Mitzi to marry him. He would put his heart out there and let her decide. With each passing mile, Keenan realized it would be wrong to put her in that position. Regardless of what Bill thought, Mitzi deserved better than him.

Her husband list had been carefully constructed, drawn to include all the characteristics that made up the man of her dreams.

He hadn't even made the top ten.

For a while, he'd thought if she was willing to give him a chance, he'd work hard and be the successful man she deserved. But if Mrs. Van Ness had her way, he'd have to leave Jackson Hole to build that successful aviation career. Trouble was, he wanted to stay.

He'd spent too many years away already. He wanted to watch his nephew grow up and spend time with his sister and friends. He could build a comfortable life here, but without being able to fly, he couldn't soar.

The door swung open and there she stood, the woman he loved.

Instead of a welcoming smile, her lips formed a grim line. Her eyes flashed blue fire. Then her gaze dropped to the flowers.

His stomach roiled as a long-buried memory from the past hit him with the force of a sledgehammer. Long ago, he had given a woman flowers. Or tried to...

Keenan thrust the flowers out stiff-armed. "These are for you."

She stared at the orange and red roses mixed with a handful of lilies. For one heartbeat. Then two.

When she took a deep breath, Keenan braced himself.

"These are lovely. Thank you." Mitzi looked up then. She cleared her throat and motioned him inside. "Let me get these in water."

Keenan expelled the breath he didn't realize he'd been holding and followed her into the kitchen. On the way, Bitty jumped down from the sofa and padded after him. He took a seat on one of the barstools and watched Mitzi arrange the flowers in a clear glass vase.

Even dressed simply in black knit pants and a fluffy blue sweater, Mitzi was the most beautiful woman he'd ever known. Yet, it wasn't simply her outer beauty that captivated him. She was just as lovely on the inside.

A woman like her deserved a successful man, not one without two nickels to rub together and a shaky future.

Once the flowers had been arranged to her apparent satisfaction, Mitzi turned to face him. She rested her back against the granite countertop and met his gaze. The blue eyes that had been stormy when she'd opened the door were now calm as glass. "We need to talk."

He nodded, gathering his storming emotions close. He thought he'd been prepared. He hadn't taken into account this intense desire—this need—for her and the life they'd begun to build together.

He'd known better than to let himself believe someone so wonderful could be his, yet he realized he'd let himself hope.

Now he had to convince her he didn't care. A nearly impossible feat, considering he'd never wanted anyone as much as he wanted her.

It's not about you, Keenan reminded himself. It was about what was best for her, for the woman he loved.

"I don't understand," she began, "why you didn't return my calls. I was worried. Why did I have to learn from Kate that you were at Wally's celebrating Joel's birthday?"

Her tone was reasonable, but her imploring look sliced like a

HER KIND OF HERO | 191

knife. Blood seeped from the fresh gash in his heart. *Make it quick,* he told himself. "Time got away from me."

Her jaw lifted as her gaze skewered him. "Why didn't you call?"

He lifted a shoulder in a careless shrug. "I got tied up with some things."

She hissed out a breath.

"So tied up you couldn't answer your phone?" The control on her voice snapped. "So tied up you couldn't call me back?"

While he might yearn to rush to her, to gather her in his arms, to apologize for his thoughtless behavior, he couldn't allow any crack to mar the insolent facade he'd affected. She must believe he didn't care.

Keenan stayed seated and shrugged again.

"When you love someone, you owe them consideration, you—"

"Who said anything about love?" Though Keenan's heart slammed against his ribs, his tone was slightly bored.

"I did." Mitzi took a deep breath, lifted her chin, met his gaze. "I'm in love with you, Keenan. I've known it for some time, but wasn't sure how to tell you."

Joy leapt but he tamped it down and merely continued to stare.

Mitzi gave a little laugh. "Ah, this is your cue to say you love me, too."

The words churned inside him, but Keenan kept his lips clamped tight. He would show her how much he loved her...by letting her go.

He rose on legs that trembled. "I enjoyed spending time with you but love wasn't part of the deal. Only friendship. Remember?"

"Friends? That's all I was to you? All I *am* to you?" Her voice rose and cracked.

"I never had a better friend than you." The stampede of

emotion welling up inside him clogged his voice. Kennan knew if he said more, he'd give himself away. Still, he leaned over and clumsily pressed his lips to her forehead. "Goodbye, Mitzi."

Without looking back, he strode out the door and felt his heart split in two.

~

For Mitzi, the next few days were a blur. She worked hard, thankful for a busy surgery schedule and heavy patient load. She did her duty and showed Noah around town. He was a nice guy but when he asked if he could take her to dinner as a thank-you, she declined.

Her chest ached with a cold, dry pain that made her feel numb inside. Keenan hadn't simply been a part of her life, he'd been her life. How would she go on without him?

For so many years she'd fought hard to get what she wanted. Her hard work and determination had paid off. She was a successful physician with a promising career. She had friends. But the life that had once seemed so rich and full, now felt hollow and empty.

She wanted more than a successful career and a comfortable life. She wanted love. Keenan's love. She wanted to share her life with him, to have his babies, to grow old with him.

The only problem was he didn't want her in the same way.

Mitzi glanced at the red dress lying across the bed. She'd purchased it weeks ago in anticipation of the awards ceremony at the Spring Gulch Country Club. When she'd tried it on, she'd envisioned accepting the award then going home and having the man she loved peel the sexy form-fitting cocktail dress off her, inch by inch.

He'd tease, she'd offer a scathing reply and they'd laugh, caught up in the conversational byplay they both enjoyed so much. They'd been perfectly matched. Or so she'd thought. Now he was out of her life.

She straightened her shoulders, thankful Keenan wouldn't be at the event tonight. Mitzi knew it was going to take all the strength she possessed simply to get through the evening.

She would do it.

She had no other choice.

CHAPTER TWENTY

Even when the walls of his boardinghouse room closed in around Keenan, he couldn't summon the energy to leave. The past three days had been hell. He'd gone to work and come home. That was the best he could manage to do. Now it was the weekend and he didn't have to go anywhere.

He hadn't heard from Steve. The logical conclusion was that his conversation with Mrs. Van Ness had gone as expected. Keenan was out. Steve just hadn't decided how to break the news to him.

Keenan had once thought flying was his whole world. He'd been wrong. Mitzi was his world.

Though he'd been physically alone in that motel room in Nebraska, Mitzi had still been with him. He'd known when he returned to Jackson Hole, she'd be waiting.

Not anymore.

He'd made the right choice. She deserved better than a mutt without a pot to pee in. A nobody. Though she hadn't personally stomped on his heart, it had ended up bruised and battered all the same.

HER KIND OF HERO | 195

A knock sounded, followed quickly by another, more forceful one. Keenan frowned. He wasn't expecting anyone.

He opened the door and found his sister standing in the hall, a garment bag slung over her arm.

Betsy brushed past him, not waiting for an invitation. "I don't have much time. Ryan is down in the car with Nate. When I picked up Ry's tuxedo, the clerk mentioned you hadn't gotten yours yet, so I had her give it to me."

Pushing newspaper pages aside, she laid the tux carefully on the bed then turned to face him.

"You look horrible." Her brows pulled together in concern. "Have you been eating?"

"I've been eating just fine." Keenan saw no need to tell her his appetite had vanished. "Sorry you went to the trouble to deliver the tux. Since I'm not going tonight, I don't need it."

"Why not?"

"There's no reason for me to be there."

He thought about mentioning Cassidy had asked him to go with her, but decided that didn't matter.

Though she said she was short of time, Betsy suddenly didn't appear in any hurry to leave.

"Kate mentioned you and Mitzi aren't together." His sister put a hand on his arm. "What happened, Keenan? I thought things were good."

Keenan wished he could find out how Mitzi was holding up. The hurt he'd seen in her eyes, the knowledge that he'd put the pain there, haunted him. "Mitzi got it in her head she loved me. Have you ever heard anything so crazy?"

"Let's make sure I got this straight." Betsy brought a finger to her lips. "Mitzi confessed she loved you and you rabbited."

"I did not *rabbit*. What kind of word is that, anyway?"

"Obviously you did, or you and Mitzi would be on your way to living happily ever after right now, instead of you being holed

196 | CINDY KIRK

up in this tiny room looking like death warmed over. Give me the deets."

"Deets? Sheesh, Bets, what are you, fifteen?"

His sister stared at him. "You might as well spill your guts. I'm not leaving until you do."

Keenan strode to the small window that overlooked Main Street. He knew all too well his little sister's stubborn streak. "It's not rocket science. Mitzi wanted more. I wanted to stay friends. That's all. Now, will you leave?"

"Bull. Pure bull." Betsy crossed the room to him. "I'll tell you how it really went down. You love Mitzi but decided she deserves someone better than you."

He gave an unsteady laugh and kept his focus out the window and away from Betsy's discerning gaze. "She does deserve better."

"Did you know I turned Ryan down the first time he asked me to marry him?"

Keenan turned. Blinked. His sister loved Ryan, had always loved Ryan. He couldn't imagine her turning down his proposal.

"I told myself his future would be hurt by me being involved in his life. I didn't feel I was worth loving." Tears sprang into Betsy's eyes. She quickly blinked them back. "Mom did a number on you and me, Keenan. The only way I was able to push her permanently from my head was to realize I deserved to be happy. Being happy is the best revenge."

Betsy wrapped her arms around him, rested her head against his shoulder. "Don't let her hurt you anymore. You're a wonderful man. You'll make a fabulous husband. If you love Mitzi, tell her the truth then let her decide. You know you can make her happy in a way no other man can. And I believe she'll make you happy, as well. The rest is just economics and pride."

After his sister left, Keenan went to the closet and took out his work jacket. Inside the zippered pocket was the small velvet box he'd been carrying around for almost a week. Keenan snapped the lid open.

Mounted high in white gold, the topaz engagement ring caught the light. He traced a finger along a band that had a decidedly art deco feel with its scrollwork and milgrain edges. Diamonds were traditional, but they were also expensive. Neither he nor Mitzi would ever call themselves traditional.

Besides, wasn't it the love and thought behind the ring that mattered? Mitzi had mentioned blue topaz was her favorite stone. And love, well he had that in abundance. Betsy was right. He'd be honest with Mitzi about his feelings and situation. She could decide where they went from here.

After tonight he'd either be the happiest man in Jackson Hole or—

Keenan shoved the negative thought from his head. Regardless of the outcome, it was long past time Gloria's reign of terror came to an end.

He set the jeweler's box on the dresser and picked up his phone.

"Cassidy," he said when she answered. "Do you still need an escort for tonight?"

Keenan arrived at the small apartment Cassidy had over her shop precisely at six-thirty. As Cassidy was being honored for her promotion of the "Locks for Love" program and for her wig-fitting services for chemotherapy patients, she didn't want to be late.

When the door swung open, Keenan released a low whistle.

Cassidy had pulled her blond hair up in some sort of twist, the style accentuating her large blue eyes. Her yellow cat-eye glasses with black polka dots provided a nice foil to the skintight black dress that showed her curvy figure to full advantage.

Though he wasn't attracted to her, Keenan admitted she

looked hot. Impulsively, he leaned over and kissed her cheek. "The men will be fighting over you tonight."

"You're a sweetie pie." Cassidy patted his cheek and tossed a feathery red boa over her shoulder. She gave an exaggerated shiver. "I can feel it. Tonight's going to be something special."

"I'd say your intuition is spot on." Keenan held out an arm. "It's a big deal for you to receive one of the Medical Foundation awards. They don't just give those out to anyone."

She smiled and took his arm. "Like I said, something special is in the air tonight."

Noah cornered Mitzi the second she'd strolled through the large double doors of the Spring Gulch Country Club. She realized she was one of the few people the man knew, but she wasn't feeling particularly charitable and definitely not in the mood for small talk.

Still, she let him compliment her on her red cocktail dress and allowed him to fetch her a glass of champagne. They spent a few moments talking about the town and various residents. He brought up Clippety Do-Dah, which she thought odd, but she knew Cassidy was also receiving an award tonight and figured he must have seen the name of her salon in the brochure.

"Cassidy is very involved in the community," she began, then smiled. "In fact, there she is with—"

Mitzi's breath stuck in her throat.

"She's with your friend Keenan." Noah's eyes turned sharp and assessing. "Are they dating?"

"I don't know." Mitzi's mind went blank. She found herself stumbling over the words. "I don't know."

She'd always prided herself on her control, but at the moment whatever tenuous hold she had was close to snapping.

Keenan wore a tux. She'd never seen him in black tie before

HER KIND OF HERO | 199

and it suited him. She waited for him to look her way but his gaze was firmly focused on Cassidy. His hair had been cut since she'd last seen him and the blue tips were history. The strands were still long and slightly wavy.

She pressed her lips together at the thought of Cassidy running her fingers through Keenan's silky hair.

Keep your hands off my man, Mitzi wanted to call out. She resisted the almost overwhelming urge to get in Cassidy's face and make her feelings perfectly clear.

She didn't move a muscle. She wasn't that streetwise girl from East L.A. anymore. And Keenan wasn't her man.

But, oh, how she wished things could be different.

"Are you going to introduce me to her?"

Mitzi jerked her head back, caught the amused look in Noah's eyes.

"Perhaps later." She forced a breezy tone. "I have some other matter to see to right now."

Mitzi pivoted on her skinny heels and sauntered in the opposite direction of Keenan and his "companion." It certainly hadn't taken long for him to jump back into the dating pool. Though her insides were tied in knots, as Mitzi crossed the large ballroom she smiled and made light conversation with anyone who stopped her. After all, she didn't want to look as if she was running from...anyone.

She'd spent enough time in the building to know that the ladies' lounge off the ballroom entrance would already be crowded. She needed quiet, a place to settle herself, to get her emotions in check, before the evening was in full swing.

Mitzi chose the lounge near the back veranda specifically because of its out-of-the-way location. There she could relax in one of the comfortable chairs and enjoy her glass of champagne.

The second she stepped into the room, she came to an abrupt stop. *Cassidy.*

The woman looked amazing in black dress and sparkly heels.

The red boa was a nice accent piece, as was the pencil-thin crimson streak running through her hair.

Cassidy twirled her boa in a motion that reminded Mitzi of Bitty's tail. In someone less confident, the gesture might have been construed as nerves.

"I thought you might be headed in this direction," Cassidy said.

"Did you?" Mitzi's kept her tone cool.

"I saw how you looked at me when I walked through the door with Keenan." A twinkle danced in Cassidy's eyes. "Admit it. You wanted to punch me."

Despite herself, Mitzi couldn't stop her lips from quirking up. Trust Cass to give it straight.

"I may have considered giving you a jab or two," Mitzi admitted, then offered an exaggerated sigh. "Yet, I let you live."

"That's because you haven't yet decided how to best make me pay," Cassidy said in a matter-of-fact tone. She gestured to a couple of upholstered barrel chairs and took a seat. "Let's discuss it."

Curious, Mitzi sat, crossed her legs and took a sip of champagne.

Almost immediately, Cassidy's gaze narrowed on the glass. "How is it?"

"Very good."

"I take it you're not into sharing?"

Mitzi gave a dry chuckle and passed the glass to her. "You might as well take that from me, too."

"Keenan is miserable." Cassidy merely took a sip of champagne. "Wow. This is good stuff."

"What do you mean, he's miserable?"

"He isn't happy about whatever happened between the two of you."

"It was his choice." Emotion thickened Mitzi's voice. "He's the one who walked away."

Cassidy leaned back in her chair, studied Mitzi as if seeing her for the first time. "And you're going to just let him waltz away from you? Girlfriend, I thought you had more spunk."

"I don't run after a man who doesn't want me. He doesn't love me, Cass. He told me."

Cassidy brayed a laugh and downed the rest of the liquid in her glass. "You bought that lie?"

Shards of hope rose inside Mitzi. She met Cassidy's gaze.

"You know what you have to do." Cassidy pulled to her feet. "While you're getting in his face, I'm going to get some champagne."

Mitzi found Keenan with Tripp and Cole. Cole gave her a welcoming smile. Tripp's faded when he saw her. Keenan's eyes turned watchful.

"If I could have a minute of your time..." Mitzi spoke directly to Keenan as if the others weren't there and pretending not to gawk.

"I take it Kate told you I was looking for you," Keenan said.

Mitzi frowned. "I haven't seen her this evening."

"Oh," he said, looking suddenly perplexed.

"We need to talk."

"Where?"

"This way." She gestured vaguely with one hand. While crossing the room, she'd considered her options. "Let's go out on the veranda. It might be a bit cool but it'll be private."

He walked beside her on their way to the patio doors, close enough that she could smell his familiar woodsy scent and feel the heat radiating from his body. When he made no move to touch her—or initiate a conversation—her heart sank.

The outside air was a few degrees cooler than when she'd arrived, but Mitzi relished the cool breeze against her hot cheeks.

202 | CINDY KIRK

She took a deep breath and turned so she faced him head-on. "I realize I'm far from perfect—"

"Mitzi, don't—"

"You need to know I've been called an arrogant, self-absorbed person who thinks she's too good for everyone else." Mitzi was determined not to sugarcoat. If he eventually chose to be with her, he had to know what he was getting. "My mother thinks I'm uppity. She—"

"Stop. Right. There." Keenan's hazel eyes flashed. "I won't tolerate lies."

"Facts. Not lies."

"Lies," he repeated, his gaze fixed on hers. "If you were relaying facts, you'd talk about a girl who overcame tremendous odds to achieve her dream. A girl who did it by focusing on her goal, by not letting anything or anyone deter her. I say she's justifiably proud of her accomplishments, not uppity."

Tears stung the backs of Mitzi's eyes but she refused to let them fall. "If you think I'm so great, why walk away from me?"

Before answering, he took off his jacket and handed it to her. Mitzi slid her arms into the coat sleeves, still warm from his body. As the heat enveloped her and his fingers lingered on the coat's lapels, some of the tightness around her heart eased.

"There's so much I need to tell you." A muscle in his jaw jumped. "Problem is, I don't know where to begin."

Seeing the distress on his face, Mitzi pushed aside her pride and touched his hand. "No rush."

His fingers curved around hers and her heart began to thump. Being with him like this felt so right. She listened as he relayed what had transpired the afternoon he'd returned from Nebraska.

Anger rose in Mitzi and spilled over into her voice. "Did that horrid woman pull her business? Did Steve wimp out and fire you?"

"I haven't heard from him." Keenan leaned over and surprised

HER KIND OF HERO | 203

her with a gentle kiss on the mouth. "I love you, Mitzi. So much I can hardly bear it."

"You said all you wanted to be was friends," she reminded him.

"That was a lie. I'd convinced myself you deserved a more successful man. If Steve lets me go, if I can't get another job flying, I may have to move. I don't want to leave Jackson Hole. But if I stay, I'll never be the successful man you deserve—"

"What is wrong with you?" Mitzi swatted his arm. "You are a success in every way that matters to me. You raised your sister when you were only a kid yourself. You gave up a college scholarship so you could stay around and watch over her. The only reason you went to prison was because you tried to help a man you didn't even know."

"Tell me how you really feel," he said, but he was smiling.

"I'm proud of you." She met his gaze, hoping he could see in her eyes all that was in her heart. "If you need to move to be happy, I'll move with you. If you want to stay, we'll stay. As long as we're together, I'll be happy."

He touched her hair as if needing the contact. "You are what Gloria told me I didn't deserve and what I'd never have."

"From what you've told me about the woman, your mother doesn't sound like someone whose opinions deserve to be given much credence."

He chuckled. "Fact."

This time it was Mitzi who needed the contact. She rested her hand on his arm. "What is it you want, Keenan?"

"I want you," he said without hesitating. "I love you, Mitzi. While I may not possess all the qualities on your husband list, I know I can make you happy."

"Ah, about that list... That's been revised recently. I happen to have the latest version in my purse." She opened her bag and pulled out a single sheet of paper. "Let me read it to you."

He opened his mouth then shut it, gave a jerky nod.

"These are the *essential* qualifications."

Keenan drew in an audible breath, his eyes wary. "I'm ready."

"Pilot."

A look of startled surprise crossed his face. "I'm a pilot."

She nodded firmly. "Criteria met."

"Loves cats."

Confusion crossed his face before an impish gleam filled his eyes. "Bitty and I are practically BFFs."

"That's because you sneak her kitty treats." Mitzi smiled. "Criteria met."

"Is that all?"

"One more." Mitzi paused.

He cocked his head.

She took a deep breath and plunged ahead. "Name must be Keenan McGregor."

His grin returned. "Why, that happens to be my name."

She handed the paper to him. "You scored one hundred percent."

"A score that pushes me to the top of your husband list."

She gazed at him through lowered lashes. "Why yes, it does."

"Riding on that high..." Keenan reached inside the jacket she wore and pulled a tiny box from an inside pocket. Then, firmly taking her hand, he dropped to one knee.

Her heart stopped. Completely stopped. The only way she knew for certain she was alive was she could hear her ragged breathing.

"From the moment I first saw you, I was captivated. When I got to know you, I realized we fit. I don't know how else to say it. We're stronger, happier, better together. If I had a list, it'd be a short one because there would be only one thing on it, and that would be your name. You, Mitzi Sanchez, are the only woman I'll ever want, the only woman who can make my life complete, the only one I'll ever love."

Tears of joy slipped down her cheeks.

HER KIND OF HERO | 205

Keenan flipped open the box and took out the beautiful blue topaz ring. "Will you do me the honor—and make me the happiest man on the planet—by agreeing to become my wife?"

"Yes," she said, and he slipped the ring on her finger. "Yes. A thousand times, yes."

Keenan rose and pulled Mitzi into his arms just as the French doors opened.

Cassidy surveyed the scene and her bright red lips lifted into a smile. She sighed lustily, took a huge gulp of champagne then lifted the now-empty glass in a toast. "Here's to true love and happy endings."

Keenan looked at Mitzi, at the woman he loved who miraculously loved him back. He tightened his hold on her and laughed with pure joy. "I couldn't put it better myself."

EPILOGUE

Mitzi's wedding day dawned bright and sunny in Jackson Hole. Though she knew she could have had a big ceremony, once she and Keenan decided to do it, they wanted to be married *now*. If it had been just up to them, they'd have headed off that night for Las Vegas.

But this wasn't just about them. This was an occasion for family and friends to gather and celebrate. When Mitzi had told Kate and Betsy over a lunch at Hill of Beans that they were thinking of a January wedding, Kate had been stunned. Who got married in January?

Mitzi had smiled.

Betsy had reminded Kate that this couple had never been traditional.

"You look beautiful," Kate told Mitzi, adjusting her dress.

Though the small wedding had turned into two hundred guests, the only things Mitzi wanted was a slinky gown and for Keenan to wear a black tux. When she'd told Keenan that just seeing him in black made her want to jump him, he'd laughed and told her black was his new favorite color.

HER KIND OF HERO | 207

"You look perfect." Betsy's eyes shimmered with tears as she stepped back to survey her almost-sister-in-law.

Mitzi felt beautiful and surprisingly calm. A serene peace had settled around her shoulders when she'd slipped on the dress. A feeling of rightness. This was what she was meant to do and Keenan was the man meant to journey with her down this path. She knew it in her heart. She knew it in her soul.

The sound of the organ filled the small waiting area off the main seating area. Her stomach jittered with anticipation.

"Almost show time." Resplendent in her emerald-green dress, identical in color to the one Betsy wore, Kate leaned over and lightly kissed Mitzi's cheek. "All happiness, dear friend."

Mitzi blinked away sudden tears. She was doing a good job keeping them in check until Betsy took her in a fierce hug.

"I always wanted a sister," Betsy whispered. "I'm so glad it's you."

"I love you both." Mitzi's voice grew thick with emotion as she thought of the upcoming years and all the good times they'd share.

She'd have left Jackson Hole if that was what Keenan wanted, or needed to do, for his career. But Mrs. Van Ness had not only reconsidered her decision and asked to have him fly for her company, she'd apologized.

Mitzi thought someone had to have intervened for such an about-face, but Keenan couldn't think who had that clout. Regardless, Jackson Hole would remain their home, and Mitzi couldn't be happier.

"Are you ready?" Betsy asked.

"I don't have my veil on yet." Mitzi glanced around the small room. "Where is it?"

"Cassidy was fooling with it." Kate pulled her brows together. "I'll see—"

Before Kate could go in search of her other bridesmaid, Cass walked through the door. It wasn't the headdress with veil Mitzi had selected. It was—

Mitzi's breath caught. "A tiara."

Cassidy grinned. "Keenan wanted to surprise you. He said you always wanted a tiara. He hoped it'd make the day extra special."

Love welled up in her already full heart and spilled over in tears. He knew her so well.

"Hey, hey." Cassidy rushed over, now alarmed. "No crying. You'll ruin your makeup."

"I'm just so ha-appy." Mitzi sniffled then accepted the tissue Betsy handed her.

"The way everyone should be on their wedding day." Cassidy's tone may have been matter-of-fact, but her eyes held the sheen of tears.

Once the tiara and veil were secured, Cassidy straightened her own green gown and listened for the music. "I believe that's our cue to line up."

Cassidy started down the aisle first, a curvy blonde scattering rose petals like a fairy nymph. Kate and Betsy flanked each side of the bride.

Mitzi saw her mother, sister and nieces sitting in the family pew at the front of the church. Her mother held Nate. About time they had a little boy in the family, she'd told Mitzi.

The rest of the sanctuary was filled with friends and colleagues. Even Mrs. Van Ness was there, sitting beside Bill and his family.

She had no hard feelings toward the woman, Mitzi realized. In fact, her actions and the resulting turmoil had allowed her and Keenan to grow closer as a couple and embrace what was truly important.

At the end of the aisle was what truly mattered. Keenan McGregor. The man who was not only her friend and lover but would soon be her husband, for all eternity.

Her hand rose to touch the tiara and she saw his smile widen.

She glanced at the ring on her hand, the one linking her love to his.

Mitzi couldn't imagine a more perfect wedding day. She had a tiara on her head, a blue stone on her finger and her very own prince waiting with love in his eyes.

The perfect prescription, she thought, as she took her first step down the aisle, for living happily ever after.

Thank you so much for spending time with Mitzi and Keenan. It warmed my heart to see how Keenan's friends had never lost faith in him and supported him in his darkest hour. He and Mitzi were such a fun couple and I was happy to share their story with you.

If you've fallen in love with Jackson Hole and the wonderful people who live there, you're going to love A DOCTOR'S PROMISE.

This book is a reader favorite and Tim, Cassidy and the twins hold a special place in my heart. This book goes beyond Tim and Cassidy's love story. It's also a story of a family being formed and love blossoming despite many obstacles. Fans of uplifting romance LOVE this book and I know you will too.

Dive into this heartwarming romance now OR keep reading for a sneak peek.

SNEAK PEEK OF A DOCTOR'S PROMISE

Cassidy Kaye knew the instant Tim Duggan walked into the Green Room. Though she was busy doing hair for those participating in the Jackson Hole Bachelor/Bachelorette Auction, her spidey senses never failed to alert her whenever the handsome doctor was nearby.

Out of the corner of her eye, she saw him pause in the doorway, a tall man with a thatch of hair the color of mahogany. His hair was cut stylishly short above a face with a strong jaw and straight nose. His hazel eyes looked green at the moment, but she knew they could turn a mesmerizing golden brown in a heartbeat. He was boyishly handsome, down to the sprig of freckles across the bridge of his nose.

His gaze scanned the room, his expression solemn.

When she'd first heard Tim would be filling in for his friend Liam Gallagher, she'd been stunned and disbelieving. Unlike the other bachelors up for bid this evening, Tim was a family man, a widower with twin seven-year- old daughters. He certainly wasn't a party animal. Other than escorting librarian Jayne Connors to a few social events now and then, he didn't even date.

When his gaze settled on her, something that looked almost like relief lifted his lips and she felt warm all over.

"Back in five," she told Zippy Rogers, a young woman whose thick dark hair practically begged to be placed into a sexy twist.

Cassidy wove her way through the small area just off the main ballroom of Spring Gulch Country Club, loving the energy in the air. With each step closer to Tim a different kind of excitement filled her. Embracing the sensation, she sidled up to him.

"Hi." Cassidy cursed the odd breathlessness that attacked her whenever he was near. To compensate she offered him a cheeky grin. "Word on the street is you're up for bid on the meat market tonight."

He winced.

She could almost see his mind spinning like a hamster wheel as he attempted to come up with the proper response to her not-so-proper comment.

"Liam had an allergic reaction." He shifted from one foot to the other. "Right now his face is puffed up like the Incredible Hulk."

Liam, an all-around nice guy, was a child psychologist who'd recently returned to Jackson Hole to set up practice. Cassidy felt a stirring of sympathy. "Poor guy."

"He hated to back out at the last minute."

"If he resembles the Hulk, it was a wise move," Cassidy said matter-of-factly. "For these events, handsome, not hulk, is what brings in the money."

Tim's gaze lingered for a moment on the pretty blondes, sensual brunettes and one dazzling redhead getting their hair and makeup done. It slid to the group of young men standing together talking.

Other than Liam-the-absent, the guys on the chopping block tonight weren't his buds. These men were businessmen and ski industry people, at least five or six years younger than Tim. His social circle—and hers—was composed primarily of medical

SNEAK PEEK OF A DOCTOR'S PROMISE | 213

professionals and young entrepreneurs with a few attorneys and social workers tossed into the mix.

Cassidy fell into the entrepreneur bucket. She owned a successful hair salon—Clippity Do Dah—in downtown Jackson. In the past year she'd expanded into doing hair, nails and makeup for events, such as weddings and other special occasions.

"I'm not sure exactly what I'm supposed to do." Tim shoved his hands into his pockets and rocked back on his heels. "Liam just told me to show up."

"Lexi Delacourt is coordinating tonight's fund-raiser. You know Lexi."

"Of course." The lines of strain on Tim's face eased.

Lexi was a mutual friend. She was also as classy and elegant as they came. The pretty social worker brought that class and elegance to anything she touched, which meant the auction wouldn't be sleazy. Or at least as non-sleazy as bidding on another human being could be.

"I'll take you to her." Cassidy looped her arm through his, congratulating herself on so quickly finding a reason to touch him.

As always, being this close sent blood coursing through her veins like warm honey. Though Cassidy normally preferred bright colors and flash, Tim's brown trousers and cream-colored shirt suited her just fine. In fact, on him she found the subdued colors incredibly sexy.

Cassidy glanced down, wondering if he liked her bright orange skirt that resembled a tutu—complete with tulle— topped by a clingy lime tee. The outfit was one of her faves.

"This way." Cassidy tugged on his arm.

His feet remained firmly planted. "You're busy. I don't want to interrupt."

Cassidy looked at him blankly.

Tim gestured toward Zippy, who was busily applying another layer of color to her mouth.

214 | SNEAK PEEK OF A DOCTOR'S PROMISE

Cassidy approved of the young woman's efforts. After all, could lips ever be too red?

"No worries." She tugged again, more firmly this time, and he moved with her, the faint intoxicating scent of his cologne teasing her nostrils. "Zippy is the last woman up, so I have plenty of time."

He nodded. "I just didn't want to disturb you."

She smiled to herself. What would he say if she told him everything about *him* disturbed *her,* but in only the very best of ways? Cassidy barely resisted the urge to ask. Instead, she steered the conversation in another direction. "How are Esi and Elle?"

Tim cocked his head and stared as if she'd spoken a language he hadn't yet mastered.

"Oh, you mean Esther and Ellyn." Warmth filled his eyes the way it always did whenever he spoke of his daughters. "They're well. Spending the evening with Grandma and Grandpa."

"I bet your mother had a coronary when she heard you were filling in for Liam tonight."

Cassidy didn't have to be a fly on the wall to know how that discussion had gone down. Suzanne Duggan, retired school-teacher, helicopter grandmother and all-around pain in the butt would never approve of her doctor son participating in anything as gauche as a bachelor auction, even if it was for a good cause.

"She didn't say much."

Tim may have kept his tone offhand but Cassidy wasn't fooled. Mama bear had definitely given him a few hard swipes of her tongue.

"What did Jayne think?" This time it was *her* tone that was carefully neutral. To complete the trifecta, she paired the voice with an interested expression and a slightly raised brow.

"Jayne?"

"Jayne Connors," Cassidy prompted.

"I didn't think to mention it."

Relief surged, as sweet as a bottle of cold beer on a hot

SNEAK PEEK OF A DOCTOR'S PROMISE | 215

summer day. Obviously Tim and Jayne were still casual, though Cass had to wonder for how much longer. It was hard to miss the desire in the librarian's eye whenever her gaze landed on him. Not-so-plain Jayne clearly had Dr. Duggan in her crosshairs.

"... for such a good cause."

Cassidy realized that while her mind was tripping down the plain-Jayne path, Tim had been speaking. Thankfully, thinking on her feet was a specialty of hers. After all, as a hairdresser, she spent a lot of time on her feet.

"Raising money for the new Women and Children's Center is something I fully support," he continued. Compassion filled those hazel eyes. His caring nature was one more check in his positive column. "For such an affluent community we have so many women and children who struggle..."

For a second, her throat constricted and breathing came hard. Instead of remaining stuffed away in a rarely opened file cabinet in her head, the comment brought her own childhood front-and-square.

Cassidy plucked the disturbing memories from her head, shoved them back into the file cabinet and firmly shut the drawer. The past had no place in her life. She was all about the present and the future.

"Lexi is right there." Cassidy gestured with her free hand, wishing the auction registration desk had been farther away. She wasn't ready to release Tim back into the world. These one-on-one times were rare and the warmth of his skin beneath her fingers an unexpected pleasure.

"I should speak with Lexi." Yet he made no move to step away.

Though Cassidy sometimes wondered how she could be the only one to feel the sizzle that was so blatant whenever they stood close, she wasn't foolish enough to entertain the thought that Tim hesitated because he wanted to spend a few more moments with her. He was simply uneasy about what he'd agreed

216 | SNEAK PEEK OF A DOCTOR'S PROMISE

to do and was trying to put off beginning the process for as long as possible.

"I have this image of standing up there and not getting a single bid." He emitted a slightly embarrassed chuckle. "I'm a middle-aged dad. Who's going to bid on me?"

Tim wasn't fishing for a compliment; he wasn't that kind of guy. He obviously had no idea just how appealing he was to the opposite sex.

"You're thirty-four. You're successful. You're hot."

He laughed. "Yeah, right."

"If it will ease your mind, I'll start the bidding," she promised him. "Kick things off."

Gratitude flooded his face. "You'd do that for me?"

"Hey." She punched him in the shoulder. "We're buddies."

Okay, perhaps that was a stretch, but saying it felt incredibly good.

"You're a very nice person." His gaze lingered on her face so long that her lips began to tingle. For a second, she had this crazy thought he might kiss her.

Instead, he squeezed her shoulder and strolled off in Lexi's direction.

After Cassidy finished making Zippy even more stunning, she took a few moments to touch up her own makeup and hair.

The auction of five women and five men had already started. The order had been predetermined beginning with a female and following a female-male format. Liam, or rather Tim, would be last on the auction block.

From the laughter and applause that arose from the ballroom each time the bidding concluded for an individual, Cassidy decided it wouldn't take long to get to Tim.

Still, she lingered in front of the long mirror, taking a second

SNEAK PEEK OF A DOCTOR'S PROMISE | 217

to add a touch more orange-marmalade gloss to her mouth before fluffing her hair with her fingers. For the evening festivities, she'd resurrected the true blond of her childhood then tipped the ends with royal blue to match the color of her eyes.

Though she often wore glasses in vivid hues or patterns, the frames were a fashion accessory rather than a necessity. Tonight she'd left them in the small apartment over her shop, the place she now called home.

Cassidy smiled broadly, making sure there were no lipstick smudges on her teeth. Satisfied, she sauntered into the ballroom on five-inch heels.

After obtaining a number for bidding, she secured a spot halfway back from the stage and watched the spirited bidding for a date with Zippy. Mr. Business Exec with the receding hairline and Mr. Snowboarder with the sun- streaked shaggy hair both seemed equally determined to win a date with the beautiful attorney.

Zippy was the last woman on the list. The bidding reached one thousand dollars before Business Exec conceded to Snowboarder. Once the applause ended, many of those who'd stayed to watch headed to the adjacent ballroom where silent-auction items flanked the perimeter of the room and a champagne fountain anchored the center. A plethora of hot hors d'oeuvres were dispensed by waiters in black pants and white shirts, holding silver trays.

Thankfully, not everyone left in search of food and drink. Cassidy calculated at least a hundred remained in the ballroom when Lexi stepped forward to introduce Tim. The dark-haired social worker, lovely in navy chiffon, included in her introductory remarks that Tim had grown up in Jackson Hole, was a respected member of the medical community and the father of twin girls.

The young doctor's face remained calm but Cassidy wasn't fooled. He was nowhere as relaxed and confident as he appeared.

218 | SNEAK PEEK OF A DOCTOR'S PROMISE

Her fingers tightened on the numbered paddle in her hand. She'd made a promise and was ready to do her duty.

Nick, Lexi's husband and well-known family law attorney, was serving as the event's guest auctioneer. He took the microphone from his wife and his gaze scanned the audience. "Do I hear a bid of one hundred?"

For a second the room was silent. One hundred was the lowest acceptable bid. From what she'd overheard while she waited, the lowest winning bid so far had been three hundred, while eleven hundred was the night's record. Most had come in around five hundred.

Cassidy was just lifting her paddle when she saw a redhead off to her right raise hers.

She recognized the woman in the sexy black dress that hugged a taut body and emphasized ample breasts. Leila Daltry was a customer at Clippity Do Dah. She stopped by regularly to get her hair cut and for an occasional color boost. A registered nurse, the striking redhead worked in the obstetrics department at the hospital. Though she wasn't the right woman for Tim, Cassidy liked her well enough.

Nick asked for a two-hundred-dollar bid. When none was forthcoming he moved into his going once, twice speech. Cassidy stopped him by lifting her number. No way was she letting Leila get Tim that cheap.

Leila turned slowly and her cat-green eyes narrowed.

Though the RN had always been friendly enough, Cassidy absorbed the feral gleam directed her way and grinned back.

If Leila thought a hostile glance could intimidate her, she was mistaken. Cassidy Kaye ate feral cats for breakfast.

"Three hundred," Nick confirmed when Leila waved her paddle as he upped the bid.

The curious gazes of the well-dressed men and women in the room were now shifting between her and Leila. Once again, Nick upped the bid. Without even thinking, Cassidy lifted her number.

SNEAK PEEK OF A DOCTOR'S PROMISE | 219

"Four hundred is the bid," Nick called out. "Do I hear five?"

The redhead hesitated now, her gaze shifting from Tim's impassive expression to Cassidy's cool gaze. Though nurses were paid well, the cost of living in Jackson Hole was through the roof. Five hundred dollars was a lot of money.

Leila tossed her head and raised her paddle.

"We're at five hundred dollars," Nick pronounced. "Will someone give us six?"

Let it go, Cassidy told herself. Five hundred was a respectable bid.

"Going twice," she heard Nick say.

Without taking a second to talk herself out of it, Cassidy shot her hand into the air.

"We have six hundred."

Leila's head snapped around and the satisfied smirk on her face vanished. If looks could kill, Cassidy would be six feet under.

"Going once, going twice. Six hundred dollars to number ninety-eight."

It was a charitable donation, Cassidy told herself as she wrote out the check. Though she had to admit dropping that amount of money in a single night hurt.

Or rather it did until she turned and found Tim standing. Right. There.

"I'm sorry you got stuck," he said.

Normally never at a loss of words, for a second Cassidy could only stare. Her heart gave a painful twist.

"I mean, I know you were only trying to increase the bid. I can give you the money to—"

She shot out a hand, stopping him before he could say more. "You're not getting out of our date that easily. I bought you fair and square, mister."

He smiled then, a warm easy lifting of his lips that did strange things to her insides. And when he took her arm, she realized he was worth every penny.

220 | SNEAK PEEK OF A DOCTOR'S PROMISE

They strolled into the ballroom, where they both enjoyed a glass of champagne. After handing the empty glasses to a passing waiter, they wandered out onto the veranda, where the conversation shifted from mutual friends and future events to their upcoming "date."

"I'll pay for the evening." Tim's tone brooked no argument. "You pick where we go. Fair?"

Cassidy considered for a moment then nodded.

The moon bathed his face in a golden glow and a light breeze tousled his hair. He really was a great-looking guy. Not only did he have a fabulous face, his lips were firm and perfectly sculpted.

As she stared, she wondered what they would feel like, taste like...

"Sounds like we've got a deal." He stuck his hand out but she ignored it, keeping her gaze focused on his lips.

Cassidy firmly believed hesitating or second-guessing was for wimps. Stepping close, she wrapped her hands around his neck and covered his mouth with hers.

Let this fabulous romance warm your heart and make you smile today! Grab your copy now.

ALSO BY CINDY KIRK

Good Hope Series

The Good Hope series is a must-read for those who love stories that uplift and bring a smile to your face.

Check out the entire Good Hope series here

Hazel Green Series

These heartwarming stories, set in the tight-knit community of Hazel Green, are sure to move you, uplift you, inspire and delight you. Enjoy uplifting romances that will keep you turning the page!

Check out the entire Hazel Green series here

Holly Pointe Series

Readers say "If you are looking for a festive, romantic read this Christmas, these are the books for you."

Check out the entire Holly Pointe series here

Jackson Hole Series

Heartwarming and uplifting stories set in beautiful Jackson Hole, Wyoming.

Check out the entire Jackson Hole series here

Silver Creek Series

Engaging and heartfelt romances centered around two powerful families whose fortunes were forged in the Colorado silver mines.

Check out the entire Silver Creek series here

Made in United States
Troutdale, OR
09/20/2023

13059506R00137